D. Scott Rogo, a renowned psychic investigator presents an overall view on the subject of haunted houses for interested followers. Inside are first-hand investigative experiences, stories and reports of some genuine hauntings of houses, churches and people.

So read on and discover what lurks behind the pages of THE HAUNTED HOUSE HANDBOOK.

The Haunted House Handbook

by D. Scott Rogo

tempo
books

Publishers · GROSSET & DUNLAP · New York
A FILMWAYS COMPANY

THE HAUNTED HOUSE HANDBOOK

ISBN: 0-448-14668-1

A Tempo Books Original
Tempo Books is registered in the U.S. Patent Office
Published simultaneously in Canada
Printed in the United States of America

CONTENTS

PREFACE

I rarely read fiction anymore. I really used to enjoy this type of reading years ago when I was in high school, but as I grew older, my interests and reading habits changed. I started reading and learning about *true* things—things that really happened—which I found more thrilling than any science fiction tale, more spellbinding than any mystery, and more mind-blowing than any adventure story.

What were these strange new things I was learning about? Well, I began studying about people who could look right into the minds of other people and tell what they were thinking, or who could move objects without touching them just by sheer concentration; and I even read about a few people who claimed that they could contact the dead. I also began to read about people who could close their eyes and "see" what was happening in cities miles away, and about houses in which furniture would float around by itself.

All these talents and happenings are called "psychic phenomena," and the scientists who study them are called "psychical researchers" or "parapsychologists." I was about sixteen years old, a second-year high school student, when I made up my mind that I wanted to study parapsychology (the study of psychic phenomena) for the rest of my life. Briefly, parapsychologists study two major types of phenomena. The first is extrasensory perception (or ESP) and the second is psychokinesis (or mind over matter, such as moving an object without touching it). However, I soon found out that being a parapsychologist wasn't a very easy job.

To begin with, as I grew older and wiser I learned that a lot of people really like to tell tall stories about themselves. I met many people, for instance, who told me that they could read my mind. But they never seemed able to do it when I asked for a demonstration. Just as many people, I'm afraid to say, and as I soon found out, like to pull hoaxes. I also learned, as I tried to track down and test people who claimed to possess psychic powers, that these talents and phenomena were rather rare. But I searched and searched and today, eleven years later, I've succeeded in witnessing all sorts of unusual events and testing people with even more unusual abilities. For instance, one woman I tested could tell you all about yourself just by touching your watch or wallet. Another psychic I tested for six weeks straight could "send his mind" into a locked room and tell you what was inside. And I've even had some psychic experiences myself. I've also had the good fortune to study several so-called haunted houses, and I've found their mystery to be the most exciting of all. And that's why I'm writing this book.

For centuries man has been fascinated by tales of haunted houses: houses in which ghostly figures walk, eerie voices cry out, and in which furniture levitates in the air and floats to and fro. Many people don't believe that such things really exist. But they are wrong!

I know, because I've even lived in a haunted house myself.

Everything you are about to read in this book is true. I'm not going to bore you with a lot of corny campfire tales about headless spectres, murderous ghouls, or chain-rattling ghosts. Instead, I'm going to recount many accounts of well-authenticated haunted houses. You'll meet people—just like you and me—who actually saw ghosts, interacted with them, and who lived in haunted houses. You'll also meet many scientists who are currently studying haunted houses and you'll learn

2

just how they go about this strange and exciting work. I'll also be discussing how we think a house becomes haunted and what causes ghosts to appear.

However, I'm not asking you to believe everything in this book. I don't even like the word "belief." Such a concept should play little part in science. Instead, I want you to study the *evidence* that haunted houses exist. I want you to evaluate everything I say *skeptically*. Try to figure out, for example, how good the evidence really is for the strange events and phenomena I'll be writing about. Remember, many people deliberately lie about what they have seen in so-called haunted houses, or even fake them. (I've personally investigated many haunted houses over the years in which someone in the house was intentionally faking all the noises and other ghostly events in order to get publicity, or just for the fun of it.) So it's your job, as you read, to determine for yourself whether lying or fraud can account for the testimony and events I'll be presenting. I personally feel that the accounts included in this book are genuine cases of ghosts and hauntings. But you must be the final judge as I describe each case.

However, I'll have to leave you with another warning. I happen to think that the evidence for the existence of haunted house is extremely impressive. And after reading this book, I think you will agree with me.

Now you know why I read less fiction these days. Make-believe stories are fine for those who like them, but I prefer to experience mysterious and strange events first hand.

D. Scott Rogo

1. WHAT IS A HAUNTED HOUSE?

In many respects, it's very hard to exactly define the term "haunted house." After all, churches, theaters, office buildings, college libraries, and even modern apartment buildings can become haunted, too. So a "haunted house" does not necessarily have to be a house at all! Any building—or place for that matter, such as a cemetery or railroad crossing—can become haunted. Instead of trying to define what a haunted house is, we should really try to define the word "haunting." This is a much more general term.

According to most experts, a haunting can be defined as any building or place in which psychic phenomena— such as apparitions, mysterious footsteps or other noises, odors, or psychokinesis—continually occur. In other words, for a building to be considered genuinely haunted, these phenomena must be directly related to the place itself. For example, let's say that you live in a haunted house and decide to move out. If the house is really haunted, the next family who moves in should experience the same things you have. Only then could we consider the place truly haunted.

You should keep in mind, though, that there are many different kinds of hauntings. No two cases are exactly alike, and, should you ever become a ghost-hunter by profession, you might encounter very different types of phenomena in the various houses you investigate. For instance:

As you probably know, ghosts are seen in many haunted houses. There seem to be two varieties of ghosts. Sometimes they are white, vapor-like forms which only vaguely resemble human beings. These apparitions are sometimes so shadowy that you can see right through them. Yet sometimes ghosts can look very lifelike. In fact, sometimes people who live in haunted houses will even mistake their ghosts for living people at first. (That is, until they either disappear into thin air or walk right through some nearby wall.) However, ghosts aren't *always* seen in haunted houses. Sometimes ghostly *noises* will be heard instead. For example, a few years ago I tried to investigate a two-story house in which ghostly footsteps were heard climbing the hallway staircase every night. These mysterious noises were the *only* phenomenon the family ever encountered in the place. Unfortunately though, the family became so frightened that they moved out of the house before I could make a proper investigation.

In another haunted house I know of, no ghost was ever seen. Instead, disembodied voices—mumbling, screaming, sobbing, and moaning—were heard night after night. And in yet other haunted houses household furniture and knick knacks will move or fly about by themselves. So you never know what you are going to run into when you investigate a haunted house. At least, that's what I've discovered.

So before taking a more in-depth look at the subject of ghosts and hauntings, let's take a look at two different haunting cases and see how they compare and contrast with one another. These two cases will give you an idea just what finding yourself in a haunted house is actually like. The first is a case of a haunted church which was reported right here from the United States. The other concerns a haunted inn in England.

Our haunted church case was originally reported by an acquaintance of mine, the Reverend William Rauscher, who is an active psychical investigator as well as the minister of Christ Episcopal Church in Woodbury, New Jersey. Reverend Rauscher personally investigated the case and recounts it in his book *The Spiritual Frontier:*

In 1968, the Reverend Harry Collins, his wife, and their three children moved to the little New Jersey town of Mullica Hill. Reverend Collins had just become parish priest at St. Stephen's Church, so the family moved into the vicarage.* At first, the place just struck the Collinses as a typical residence, similar to the other vicarages in which they had lived before. It didn't take them long, though, to realize that there was something rather peculiar about the place despite its very normal appearance and cheery atmosphere. It seemed almost as though someone else was sharing the house with them.

"We noticed that the tablecloth in the dining room was folded back, accordion-style, when none of us had done it," Mrs. Collins told Rauscher. "This happened repeatedly when my husband and I were out, or when we were all asleep, or when we were all out and the house was empty and locked."

Soon after, they started to notice other indications that someone—or something—was playing tricks on them whenever their backs were turned. Oftentimes, for example, a couch cushion would be moved from its regular position when no one was watching. But the Collinses were down-to-earth people, and so shrugged off these minor-league mysteries. They figured that, since they were only occasional happenings, they really weren't worth paying too much attention to. They even blamed the disturbances on their pet cats.

However, the haunting became more active a year and a half later. Now a ghostly odor began to invade the house. Not only did Reverend and Mrs. Collins smell the puzzling aroma, but their fifteen-year-old son did too. He thought it smelled like mosquito repellent. And, for that matter, so did his parents. The odor was most

---

*A vicarage is that part of a church in which the minister or priest lives.

often manifested in the living and dining rooms and no one could find any explanation for it. Everyone was completely baffled. And just as the Collinses came up with a possible solution to the mystery—that the odor was somehow coming from the plaster on the walls—new odors began to haunt the quarters. Sometimes it smelled as if food were being cooked in the vicarage, although the kitchen would always be found deserted and unused when the perplexed family tried to track down the aromas.

What were these weird odors leading up to? A very startled Reverend Collins discovered the answer to this puzzle on March 6, 1971, over two years after he had originally moved into the house. On that day he finally met, or at least saw, his phantom boarder.

As he told Rauscher, some friends had come to visit that evening. They were all sitting around just talking and relaxing when suddenly:

> . . . I looked up and saw it standing in the hallway leading to the dining room. It was the figure of a man. He had muddy blond hair but his features were indistinct, as though they were in a shadow. He was wearing an Eisenhower jacket, and his hands were shoved deep into the slit pockets. The figure was perfectly distinct and solid-looking down to the knees, but below that it trailed off so that I could see the floorboards through where the legs should have been.

Moments later the phantom simply faded away.

Notice in this case that only Reverend Collins saw the figure. If the phantom had been a physical being, everyone else should have seen it too. But they didn't. This would seem to prove that Reverend Collins was seeing a figure which was definitely not made of flesh and blood.

However, even though Reverend Collins was the only one to see the ghost when it first put in its appearance,

other members of the household saw it too . . . but only
on later occasions.

Mrs. Collins saw the apparition about a year after her
husband's experience. She was cleaning out a closet at
the time when she just seemed to "sense" a presence in
the room with her. On turning around, she found herself
almost face to face with the ghost. However, on this occasion, far from being semitransparent from the legs
down as Reverend Collins had seen it, the ghost was
totally lifelike. As Mrs. Collins said: " . . . He looked so
solid and lifelike that for a moment I thought he must be
a flesh and blood intruder. But unlike any intruder, the
figure just faded away."

Just who this mysterious visitor was is something the
Collinses were apparently never able to discover. At
least, Reverend Rauscher doesn't give us any hint in his
detailed account of the case.

Our second haunting case comes from Europe. This
certainly shouldn't strike anyone as odd. Haunted
houses, after all, have been recorded in every country in
the world. Even the ancient Romans and Greeks wrote
of haunted houses and ghostly visitors. For some reason, though, people do like to think of ghosts as in-
habitating only dank old castles or medieval inns. While
the following case fits the bill, so to speak, this commonly held belief is a complete misconception. There are just
as many haunted-house reports from the United States
and Canada as from the old-world countries such as
Germany, France, or England. Just as many ghosts
seem to be lurking about modern tract homes as in run-
down old castles. However, the following case does
come from Great Britain and concerns one of the many
old inns in that country which has quite a ghostly reputation.

The Queen's Head Inn is a typical English tavern. It's
an old structure, originally built in 1730, and was at one

time a farmhouse. It is still doing business in the little town of Ickesham in Sussex despite the fact that the place also plays host to a ghost. The present landlord is Mr. Charles Crundwell, who took over the ownership of the inn in 1953, and he has seen the ghost himself on one occasion. But, as he told investigators later, he had no idea that the old house was haunted when he first took it over. He also had quite a story to tell.

Crundwell first began noticing odd goings-on at the inn when he started hearing strange "knocking" sounds shortly after he moved there. He couldn't exactly isolate the source of the sounds but on one occasion at least, he claimed, the noises were made on a beer keg. Though a bit baffled, Crundwell took little interest in what was causing the noises. After all, they weren't really bothering him. It was only a few months later that he actually saw the inn's resident ghost. At the time, he was standing at the bar looking into a back room when, to his surprise, he saw a figure standing there. He looked about sixty or seventy years old, had a beard, and was dressed in the garb of years past . . . complete with tweed waistcoat and pocket watch. Mr. Crundwell glanced away for a moment, and the apparition vanished.

Later on, Crundwell learned that a former and now deceased landlord of the inn resembled the man he had seen. In fact, after his death the man had been laid in state right on the bar!

The apparition was seen again in 1958; this time by a casual visitor to the inn, Mrs. Grace Miles. She immediately wrote out an account of the incident and sent it to Andrew MacKenzie, one of Great Britain's most active and well-qualified ghost-hunters, who in turn decided to collect as much testimony about the haunted inn as he could.

Mrs. Miles and her husband were business people

who had stopped at the inn just to refresh themselves after a long drive. They barely had time to relax before Mrs. Miles saw the ghost:

> I was standing in the bar . . . It was an early summer evening and there were quite a few people in the bar. I watched the landlord approach me from another room; as he came he switched off the electric light that had been left burning. I told him there was an old man sitting in the room facing the fireplace, as I was surprised that he would switch off a light with a visitor there. I pointed to the man, whom I could still see, but nobody else could, and he faded away before my eyes.

Later, Mrs. Miles told MacKenzie that the figure was dressed in old-fashioned clothing and was bearded. As she told the investigator:

> He was about nine or twelve feet away, in profile, was wearing a hat like an old misshapen trilby,* with the brim turned down all the way round. He gave the all-over impression of dun or khaki colouring. He seemed to be wearing a loose smock-like garment, since it was tied around the waist with rope or string, not a belt. There was what looked like a piece of chain hanging by his right leg. He had muddy boots or leggings, he was elderly, bewhiskered, and with gnarled hands, and was holding a piece of straw (?) to his mouth. His feet stuck out towards the fire. He looked just like a contented shepherd or farmer relaxing. Since he was not important to me I can't say when I first saw him. I was only aware of him when the landlord was going to switch off the light. By saying it was an early summer evening I mean it was just after 8 p.m., still very light outside, but in an an-

---

*trilby: a type of soft felt hat popular in England.

cient, low-roofed house definitely dusk enough for a good landlord to switch on the lights.

Mrs. Miles also made it clear in her report that she had just been standing, not drinking, at the bar when she saw the ghost!

On checking out the history of the inn, McKenzie discovered that Mr. Crundwell's sister had also seen the apparition in the same year as Mrs. Miles's encounter. She was very upset by the incident since she hadn't thought such things were possible. From all we can gather, the inn is still haunted.

Now before proceeding any further, let's take a little closer look at these two cases. First of all, we might ask ourselves, how do they compare to each other? Obviously, both cases read somewhat alike. In each instance an apparition was seen. And also in both hauntings there was some degree of non-reality about the ghosts, since not everybody present who *should have* seen them actually did. Yet, the figures sometimes appeared so true to life that they were mistaken for living people. So these two cases should counter the commonly held myth that ghosts are whispy, chain-rattling, or moaning figures. Finally, the ghosts neither annoyed nor harassed anyone. They simply appeared out of nowhere and then vanished just as oddly.

Despite these similarities, though, there are some striking differences between the two cases. To begin with, one haunting had enough power behind it to move objects about; that is, the Reverend Collins's ghost moved a couch cushion and often folded back a tablecloth. The Queen's Head Inn's ghost apparently had no such ability. Yet, in this latter case, the haunting first made itself known by producing strange noises such as knockings and thumpings. The Collinses haunting produced odors instead.

As I said before, no two haunted houses are exactly alike. While many cases are very similar to one another, they all have their individual characteristics.

In both of the above cases, the ghosts were visible to only some people, while at the same time quite invisible to others. This fact may strike you as strange, but it is very typical of many ghosts. Sometimes it almost seems as if ghosts can choose to whom they wish to appear, and are not about to share the fun with anybody else. It might also be possible that only a few people are sensitive enough to "see" ghosts, while others are not. However, there is no hard and fast rule about this. There are several cases on record in which ghosts have appeared to whole groups of people at the same time. These are called "collective apparitions."

Just take a look at the following case which was reported by the Society for Psychical Research in 1932. The S.P.R. is a scientific organization in Great Britain (first founded in 1882) which is specifically engaged in studying and investigating hauntings, apparitions, and people who claim to have psychic abilities. It is still active today. The following case is only one of many which the S.P.R. has studied over the years. Indeed, when it was first founded, the S.P.R. leaders immediately set up a special committee just to investigate haunted houses. This case, though, has to rate as one of the more interesting ones that they were called upon to study.

This haunted house was not a very impressive place; it was just a run-down, two-story cottage in Wiltshire. The tenants were Mr. and Mrs. Edwards, their five children, and Mrs. Edwards's mother, Grandma Bull. The house was in very bad repair, for although the Edwards' were hard-working people, they were very poor. Many of the rooms were so dilapidated that they had been closed off and were not used for living quarters. One of these rooms, an upstairs bedroom, had once been the bedchamber of Grandpa Bull, but it had been closed off after his death in 1931. The house had no reputation for being haunted in any way, and the family only began to realize that they had a ghost on their hands eight months

after Grandpa Bull had passed away. It was his ghost
that had returned to haunt them.

The ghost was first seen one night in February, 1932.
It was a cold night and a perfect setting for something
supernatural to occur. The children felt nervous and apprehensive and realized that something eerie was about
to happen. Then, two of them saw the ghost for the first
time. They saw "Grandpa Bull" walk up the stairs and
enter the room which he had once occupied. They
screamed in terror when they realized they had seen a
dead man! Eventually, though, the ghost became a familiar visitor to the house. Practically everyone saw it at
one time or another, and sometimes it was seen collectively by several members of the household. This ghost,
however, didn't just appear and disappear in a matter of
seconds as some apparitions do; it would often walk
around the house and remain in full sight of everybody
for up to half an hour, and sometimes even longer. Also,
the family members would get a feeling of a "presence"
in the house before the phantom would actually appear.

Sometime later the Edwards moved to a new house,
but the ghost didn't follow them.

There are a great many unfounded myths about
ghosts and hauntings. I am sure you have already noticed that the three haunted houses cited above are very
different from the ghosts and hauntings of legend and
fiction. Ghosts aren't out to kill anybody, or avenge
their deaths. Nor do they talk or communicate with the
living, although this has been known to occur on rare
occasions. And they certainly don't appear with sheets
draped over their heads. There are many other miscon-
ceptions about haunted houses which I would like to
clear up before we delve into the subject any further. For
the present, I'll focus attention on just a few of these
myths.

First of all, just because an apparition is seen in a
house does *not* mean that the house is actually haunted.

The following example is a good case in point:

On October 29, 1976 an acquaintance of mine, whom I'll call Mrs. Berger, sent me the following account of an experience she had had just prior to her letter. She had made out her report right after the eerie event had taken place, so the incident was clear in her mind as she wrote:

Sometime during the night of October 28th, I was awakened by something—I couldn't figure out what —and looking up, sitting up in my bed, I saw in the living room between my bedroom and the den a woman's figure clad in a green caftan. I couldn't see the face since it seemed to be in a sort of haze ... I asked her what she wanted but, of course, there was no response.

At that time, Mrs. Berger, who was naturally puzzled by this unexpected visitation, got up and turned on the lights. As she did, the figure vanished. But, as Mrs. Berger continued:

I ... looked all around the house and then went back to bed, turned off the lights and reached down to pull up the sheet when I looked out into the living room again, and there was the apparition again ... The next day I had a call from my daughter-in-law, informing me that my friend Sue had passed away very suddenly from a massive coronary that morning and then it dawned on me that the person I saw was actually Sue.

Mrs. Berger informed me that, although she didn't realize it at the time of the sighting, her friend Sue did own a green caftan and often wore it. This gave her the final clue as to the identity of the apparition.

There are literally hundreds of cases just like this one on record; that is, there are many documented cases on file in which people have seen the apparitions of friends

or relatives appearing before them at the very moment
of their deaths. These instances are called "crisis apparitions" and have little to do with haunted houses. Although you might say that Mrs. Berger saw the "ghost"
of her friend, you cannot say that her house is haunted
because of it. The apparition was just an isolated psychic
event in Mrs. Berger's life, and it has never been seen
again. Now, if this apparition started to appear in Mrs.
Berger's home time and time again and over a long period of time, that would be a different matter!

Another question people often ask is whether ghosts
can be harmful. Ghosts of fiction often are, and many
people think that ghosts are invariably out to do some
harm. However, the fact remains that hauntings very
rarely hurt anyone, even though there are a few minor
exceptions. To be sure, I know of no documented haunting in which anyone has ever been killed or seriously
injured by a ghost. But every once in a while you will run
into a case or two in which the haunting acted a bit on
the brutal side. For instance, the following case was reported by the famous French astronomer Camille Flammarion in his book *Haunted Houses,* and it is a good
example of a haunting that became rather nasty:

In October of 1919 Mr. Homen Christo, a young law
student, moved into a two-story villa in the little scenic
town of Comeada, Portugal, along with his wife and a
small staff which consisted of two maids. Only a week
later, a friend of theirs, Gomez Paredes, came to visit.
He was the first to realize that the villa was haunted,
when, right after he went to bed on the first night of his
visit, he heard knocking noises on a nearby window
pane. He got up and investigated, but could find no explanation for the noises. Later that night, he heard
footsteps pacing the villa and could hear the sound of
doors opening and closing. It was a scary night, and
Paredes was no doubt relieved when daybreak came.

The next day, Paredes reported the disturbances to his
host. But Christo laughed off the incidents, and assured

his friend that he had heard nothing at all the night before. He admitted in all honesty, however, that he slept in a different part of the house and could easily have slept through any noises which were produced in his friend's part of the villa.

Despite his initial disbelief, Christo was certainly not immune to the ghost's ghastly pranks, and one night, only a few weeks later, he himself heard incredible banging sounds throughout the house. He searched the house frantically looking for an intruder, but had no luck finding any prowlers about. Then something happened which really unnerved him. The account of this haunting is so dramatic at this point that I can't help but quote from the original report:

Mr. Christo quickly descended the stairs and stationed himself by the door. The blows started afresh. He opened it suddenly, and saw nobody. He went out to ascertain whether anyone ran away down a neighboring lane. Hardly was he out when the door banged behind him and was locked. Outside he saw nobody. To return home he had to knock, and his wife came down and opened the door. Mr. Christo, much interested, was convinced that somebody had played a practical joke. He took up his revolver. "We shall see," he said.

The doors went on being shaken, and in a little room next to their bedroom, which had no exit, the noises were even louder. All this passed in complete darkness, for as soon as a light was struck nothing more was heard. Mr. Homen Christo, more and more anxious to discover the trickster, stood on the landing of the stairs leading to the ground floor, revolver in hand. Hardly had a match which he held in his fingers gone out when he heard, close to his face, a loud burst of laughter which echoed over the whole house. He saw a white cloud in front of him, and two wisps of whitish light issuing from his nostrils. It was too much! The observer felt his courage giving way. The phenomena continued more or less the same until 4 a.m.

The next day, Christo called in the police and implored them to help solve the mystery of the rapping noises. The police agreed, of course, and that night Christo and a squadron of police officers stationed themselves throughout the house. The police also heard the strange poundings but they—like Christo—could find nothing human producing them. One officer became so frustrated by the noises, and by his inability to catch anyone producing them, that he went crazy and ran around the house waving his sword and slashing it through the air. He had to be physically restrained from hurting himself!

Apparently all this commotion only infuriated the force behind the haunting. No sooner had the officer been restrained than *Christo felt a hard blow on his cheek. He screamed in pain, since it felt like fangs had dug into his flesh and had tried to rip his face off. Reddish finger marks could be clearly seen on the side of his face.*

This last attack was too much for the police, and they immediately left vowing that they would never return. The Christos soon followed.

In this case, then, the haunting actually did "attack" a member of the household. There are other cases on record in which those visiting haunted houses have been jabbed or slapped about, but these instances are very rare.* Generally, hauntings tend to be rather undramatic and almost casual affairs.

So far, ghosts were *seen* in all the episodes I've re-

---

*In Chapter 4 I will discuss "evil hauntings"; hauntings in which ghosts seem to have wicked intentions. But these cases are so rare that they may be considered exceptions to the rule. Even in these cases, though, rarely do the ghosts do anybody any genuine physical harm.

counted. This might give you yet another misconception. Not all haunted houses have visible ghosts prowling about, and, as I have already mentioned, in many cases phantoms are never seen at all, although they may be heard. I know of more than one case in which ghostly footsteps were the only manifestation the household ever experienced. In one case which Flammarion includes in his book, raps were heard, disembodied voices shrieked and wailed night after night, and objects moved by themselves or simply vanished altogether. But no phantoms were seen. So, the notion that ghosts are *always* seen in haunted places is totally unfounded.

My friend and fellow psychical investigator, Raymond Bayless, investigated one such case himself back in the 1940s.

The house was, for that time, rather modern and was located in the quiet little Los Angeles suburb of Eagle Rock. It had quite a reputation for being haunted. Bayless often visited the house to talk to the residents about the haunting. Then one day he confronted the ghost himself. He describes his encounter thus:

I was seated in the breakfast room having coffee with Mrs. X. At 5:45 P.M. we heard someone at the front door. I heard the sound of the lock mechanism in operation and the door open. Without the least thought that anything was out of the ordinary, I automatically got up from the table to see who it was.

As Bayless arose, he was stopped by his hostess. "That's only the ghost," she warned. Bayless thought at first that the woman was joking and he proceeded to walk to the living room. Although he clearly had heard the door open, he now found it tightly closed. Then, as he stood there staring, he clearly *heard* it close! But by no means was that startling occurrence the end of the encounter:

As I walked within a few feet of the door, I heard three distinct footsteps walk away from the door into the carpeted hallway. In spite of the carpeting the footsteps were very audible. They were within one and a half yards of me, and consequently were within my immediate range of vision. There was no doubt of the footsteps and there was no doubt that the walker was completely invisible. There was simply nothing to see.

I should add at this point that Raymond Bayless has been investigating haunted houses and similar phenomena for over twenty-five years and has written three books on this subject alone. In addition, he has lived in a haunted house, has investigated scores of others, and has even seen a ghost or two during the course of his career. He is probably one of the most experienced ghost-hunters in the business, so his testimony is particularly impressive.

There are two further myths about haunted houses which also should be dispelled. The first is that only old, broken-down buildings become haunted. This isn't true at all. Many relatively new homes, such as the one Bayless investigated, are just as haunted as some of the old, traditional, stately homes of England. The other myth is that ghosts can't be photographed. Quite to the contrary, there are a few well-authenticated photographs of ghosts on record.

One of the most curious of these was taken during the haunting of the S.S. *Watertown,* a large oil tanker which was owned by an oil service company in New York back in the 1920s and 1930s. The *Watertown* case is particularly interesting because we know exactly when the haunting started and who the "haunters" were.

In December 1924, the *Watertown* set sail from New York and headed for the Panama Canal. However, a tragic accident ruined the otherwise pleasant and re-

freshing trip. Two seamen, James Courtney and Michael
Tracy were overcome by gas fumes while cleaning part
of the ship and died. They were buried at sea on December 4th, and the haunting began the next day. It wasn't
the ship itself that became haunted, but the sea around
it. To the total astonishment of the crew, the faces of the
two dead men could be seen clearly in the ocean right
next to the ship. The faces followed the ship day after
day. They never failed to appear, and every member of
the crew, including the captain and first mate, saw them.
They always appeared at the same distance from the
vessel and never moved about the water. Nor did the
expressions on their faces ever change. Indeed, they
looked more like photo images than actual ghosts.

When the ship docked in New Orleans, the captain
duly reported the bizarre events to his superiors. Far
from laughing at the story, they suggested that he try to
photograph the phantom faces if they should appear
again. The idea struck the fancy of both the captain and
the first mate and they quickly agreed to the plan.

The apparitions appeared again when the ship set sail
a few days later and the first mate took six pictures of
them. He did not develop the film himself, though. Instead, he turned it over to officials of the company that
owned the *Watertown,* and they developed it. The mate
followed this procedure to dispel any notion that he had
faked the photographs. The results of the experiment
were curious, to say the least. Although five of the
photos showed nothing but empty sea, one shot clearly
showed two faces languishing in the water beside the
ship.

More "traditional" ghosts have been photographed
as well. One of these was taken at Raynham Hall in
Great Britain.

Raynham Hall is one of England's most famous
haunted houses. It is a large manor house in Nor-
folkshire, and, like so many stately British homes, it is
an old building. The house has long been the residence

of each successive Lord and Lady Townshend and has been handed down from heir to heir for many generations. Raynham Hall has also been the home of a mysterious "Brown Lady," who has been seen by several independent witnesses all the way back to 1835. Usually the ghost has been seen walking up and down the grand oak staircase of the house. In 1926, both the son of Lord and Lady Townshend and a friend claimed that they saw the ghost there. Further sightings of the ghost have been made repeatedly up until 1965.

On September 19, 1936, two photographers were commissioned by Lady Townshend to shoot a series of documentary photos of the famous house. It was a big job, so the men had to work all day. At four in the afternoon they were preparing to take a photograph of the grand staircase where the ghost has been seen so habitually. They were just getting ready to snap the picture when one of the men, Mr. Indre Shira, suddenly saw what he later described as an "ethereal veiled form" moving down the steps.

"Quick, quick, there's something! Are you ready?" were the only words he could shout to his fellow photographer.

His friend took the picture, although he couldn't see the figure himself and didn't even know what all the fuss was about. In fact, he laughed at his comrade's story. The next day, though, the photograph was developed, and a semitransparent figure had indeed been captured on the plate. The photographers were amazed.

The photograph of Raynham Hall's "Brown Lady" and the strange story behind it have not been kept secret. Both were published in the December 26, 1936 issue of *Country Life* magazine, and the photograph still remains one of the best-documented pictures of its kind.

By this time you are probably asking yourself the same question everyone who has ever been involved in parapsychology has asked himself at one time or anoth-

er. Just what force or intelligence lies behind ghosts and
hauntings? One prevalent view is that a house becomes
haunted when some tragedy, such as a death or a
murder, has occurred there in the past. This is apparently true in some cases, but not in all. Nonetheless, many
haunted places have indeed once been the scenes of violence and tragedy. To prove this point, one need only
look at a few statistics about haunted houses.

In 1919 one of Italy's leading experts on psychic
phenomena, Ernesto Bozzano, collected 374 accounts of
haunted houses from all over the world. He published
these, together with an analysis of them, in his book, *Dei
Fenomeni d'Infestazione* (this huge book has never been
translated into English, I am sorry to say). He found
that a tragic death had indeed occurred in 180 of these
houses. In 27 additional cases, no tragic deaths had ever
been recorded, but there was evidence—such as human
bones unearthed near the house—which implied that
some tragedy or misdeed had been covered up. Deaths
had also occurred in 97 additional houses, but they had
not been tragic or unusual in any way. Out of these 374
cases, ghosts were seen in 311 of them. In 76 cases, the
ghosts looked just like people who had actually lived in
the houses at one time. In 41 further cases, the figures
were not at first recognized, but were later found to resemble old portraits or photographs of previous tenants
found *after* the ghosts had been reported and described
by witnesses.

Are ghosts, then, really spirits of the dead which have
come back to haunt us? Are they somehow "chained" to
the areas where they lived and died?

This is a possibility. But it is only that . . . a theory.
There are, however, many other theories which can account for apparitions and haunted houses. Ghosts could
be, for example, "memory pictures" of the past which
habitually replay themselves for some unknown reason.
Similarly, a haunting could occur when a house begins
to discharge a sort of "psychic force" (like a pressure

cooker giving off steam) which has somehow built up in its confines.

So, as you might have guessed by now, psychical researchers don't uniformly agree on what a haunting really is, what makes a house or place that way, or just what ghosts are. Everyone has his or her own ideas on the subject. All we can do is explore and analyze case after case.

In summary, then, there are only a few general but definite things we *can* say about hauntings:

(1) The ghosts and haunted houses of fact are very different from those of fiction.

(2) A haunting can occur just about anywhere, and not necessarily solely in a house.

(3) There is no such thing as a "typical" haunted house. Although many cases resemble each other, each one will be uniquely different from any other.

(4) Hauntings can produce a wide assortment of different phenomena, including: apparitions, odd noises, odors, the feeling of a "presence" in the place, strange lights, and the unaccountable movement of physical objects.

(5) Although ghosts may actually be spirits of the dead, we have no absolute proof of this and there are many other theories which can account for apparitions and hauntings as well.

These five points might be considered a handy reference guide to what we do know for sure about hauntings.

You can readily see why the study of haunted houses and other hauntings is so fascinating and challenging. On one hand, we have collected a great amount of information on these places. Yet, on the other hand, we still don't fully understand everything about the forces and energies which actually lie behind these unusual occurrences.

2. HAUNTED HOUSES: YESTERDAY AND TODAY

In the previous chapter I pointed out that many haunted houses, even though located in different countries, will often share several common features. The same thing can be said about hauntings down through the ages. A haunted house which was reported back in the sixteenth century may have many characteristics in common with a haunting still active today. Unlike fashions in clothing, hair styles, or architecture, haunted houses have not changed over the years. These places appear to be beyond time . . . as though within their walls time itself were standing still.

With this in mind, let's take a look at a few famous haunted houses of yesteryear and compare them to some recently reported hauntings still continuing today. Although these cases resemble each other in many respects, notice the difference in the way they have been *investigated* down through the years.

One of the best-authenticated haunted houses ever investigated was reported to the Society for Psychical Research in 1892 by a young medical student who wrote under the name of Miss R.C. Morton. Her real name was Rose Despard, but she wrote her report under a false name so that neither she nor her family would be bothered by publicity or ridicule. Miss Despard moved into the haunted house in 1882 with her father, Captain Despard, her mother, three sisters, and two brothers. She was only nineteen years old at the time. But this is getting a little ahead of our story already.

The house itself was a two story, fourteen-room home

in the city of Cheltenham, England and was a typical middle-class home of the times. It had bedrooms on both floors, and a staircase led through the center of the house. The building was still rather new when the Despards originally moved in, since it had only been built in 1860. The first owner had been a Mr. Henry Swinhoe, who lived there until 1876. But those years were not happy ones for him. His wife died during their occupancy and he remarried two years later. By this time, though, the poor man had turned to drink and even taking on the responsibilities of a new marriage did little to reform him. His second wife, Imogene, did all she could to cure her husband of his terrible addiction, but instead fell victim to the bottle herself. Subsequently, their married life together was ruined by constant quarreling which sometimes ended in near violent scenes. They fought constantly over money, and over their children, and finally the new Mrs. Swinhoe got so fed up that she packed her bags and moved out. Mr. Swinhoe died only a few months later in July of 1876. Imogene Swinhoe died two years later and her remains were brought back to Cheltenham and buried a quarter mile away from the house in which she had lived.

After her death, the Swinhoe house was bought by an elderly man, who died only six months later. His widow moved out shortly afterward, and the house remained unoccupied for some four years. Then, in 1882, the Despards leased it. Already rumors that the house was haunted were spreading through Cheltenham like an uncontrolled fire.

Rose Despard, who must have been a very intelligent and brave girl, was the first to see the ghost, and she continued to see it between 1882 and 1889, the year in which the haunting began to "die out." Luckily for us, she kept detailed records of all these appearances and also kept notes on all the other phenomena she experienced in the house or which were reported to her by other family members, relatives, and visitors. So we have virtually a day-to-day diary of the Cheltenham ghost.

Although Rose Despard moved into the house in March, she didn't see the ghost until the following June:

> I had gone up to my room, but was not yet in bed, when I heard someone at the door, and went to it, thinking it might be my mother. On opening the door, I saw no one; but on going a few steps along the passage, I saw the figure of a tall lady, dressed in black, standing at the head of the stairs. After a few moments she descended the stairs, and I followed for a short distance, feeling curious what it could be.

Unfortunately, Rose's candle burned out as she started to follow the figure, so she had to return to her room. Nonetheless, she had been able to get a pretty good look at the weeping lady and subsequently recorded in her notes:

> The figure was that of a tall lady, dressed in black of a soft woollen material, judging from the slight sound in moving. The face was hidden in a handkerchief held in the right hand. This is all I noticed then; but on further occasions, when I was able to observe her more closely, I saw the upper part of the left side of the forehead, and a little of the hair above. Her left hand was nearly hidden by her sleeve and a fold of her dress. As she held it down a portion of a widow's cuff was visible on both wrists, so that the whole impression was that of a lady in widow's weeds. There was no cap on the head but a general effect of blackness suggests a bonnet, with long veil or a hood.

The crying lady did not appear very often during the first years of the Despard's tenancy. This haunting was not at all like the nightly horror that stalked the Christos's villa in Comeada, Portugal (which I summarized in the last chapter) that so frightened its occupants. Instead, Miss Despard saw her phantom friend only about six times over the next few years. But other people in the house also saw it as well.

For instance, one evening in the summer of 1882 one of Rose's sisters was walking down the central staircase when she saw a woman at the bottom of the stairs. The figure was so lifelike that she immediately mistook it for a nun. The figure walked right past her and entered a drawing room. Rose's sister never even thought for a moment that the figure was anything but a real flesh-and-blood visitor, and she was somewhat startled when she learned that no one was visiting the house that day.

During the next year the ghost was seen by a maid and by one of Rose's brothers. He and a friend had been playing outside when, glancing back at the house, they both saw a woman weeping at the drawing room window. They ran into the house "to see who it could be that was crying so bitterly," as Miss Despard recorded in her notes, but they found no one there.

However, although many members of the Despard family saw the ghost, Rose was the only one in the household willing to *investigate* the phantom. After her very first experience, in fact, Miss Despard made up her mind right then and there to follow the figure whenever she could, or try to make contact with it. Her chance came on July 19, 1884:

> I opened the drawing-room door softly and went in, standing just by it. She came in past me and walked to the sofa and stood still there, so I went up to her and asked her if I could help her. She moved, and I thought she was going to speak, but she only gave a slight gasp and moved towards the door. Just by the door I spoke to her again, but she seemed as if

she were quite unable to speak. She walked into the hall, then by the side door she seemed to disappear as before.

This little adventure hardly struck Miss Despard as a total failure, for it gave her the idea for a new experiment. She was puzzled by the fact that the ghost seemed a physically real being, but also nonmaterial at the same time. On one hand, the ghost was so lifelike that most people who saw it automatically assumed that it was a living person. Also, the ghost was able to make quite a bit of noise. Many times during these years the Despards heard strange footsteps in the house at night, or heard door handles jiggle. They actually *saw* door handles turn by themselves on a few occasions when the ghost was particularly active. Yet, the ghost was so ethereal that it had no difficulty vanishing in an instant or walking right through a handy wall.

It didn't take long for Rose to figure out a way to test whether the ghost was a physical being or not. Since the spectre often walked down the staircase steps, she merely tied strings across them! These were so delicately attached, though, that even the slightest contact would pull them down. Then, night after night, she secretly watched the staircase waiting for the ghost to appear. Would it knock down the strings or not, she wondered? The experiment was a success. On two occasions, Rose was able to watch the ghost glide right *through* the trap without upsetting the strings.

Beginning in 1884, the ghost's appearances became more and more frequent, and this gave Miss Despard the opportunity to make even more interesting observations about the phantom. For instance, she discovered that while she could often see the ghost, other people in the house could not. Some of her notes on this strange phenomenon are well worth quoting. As she recorded on July 21st:

I went into the drawing-room where my father and sisters were sitting, about 9 in the evening, and sat down on a couch close to the bow window. A few minutes after, as I sat reading, I saw the figure come in at the open door, cross the room and take up a position close behind the couch where I was. I was astonished that no one else in the room saw her, as she was so very distinct to me. My youngest brother, who had before seen her, was not in the room. She stood behind the couch for about half an hour and then as usual walked to the door. I went after her, on the excuse of getting a book, and saw her pass along the hall, until she came to the garden door, where she disappeared. I spoke to her as she passed the foot of the stairs, but she did not answer, although as before she stopped and seemed as though *about* to speak.

Yet, only two months later, on August 12th, she was able to report:

On August 12th, about 8 p.m., and still quite light, my sister Edith was singing in the back drawing-room. I heard her stop abruptly, come out into the hall, and call me. She said she had seen the figure in the drawing-room, close behind her as she sat at the piano. I went back into the room with her, and saw the figure in the bow window in her usual place. I spoke to her several times, but had no answer. She stood there for about 10 minutes, or a quarter of an hour; then went across the room to the door, and along the passage, disappearing in the same place by the garden door.

An even more peculiar event took place in July, 1885. Edith was sitting alone at the piano in the drawing-room one evening when she felt an icy-cold presence. She looked up and saw the ghost right next to her, as though

ready to turn the page of her song book. She called out
to Rose, who immediately rushed in and also saw the
ghost. But by this time the ghost had become totally
invisible to Edith!

Judging by Miss Despard's letters and notes, these
months must have been very active ones for the ghost.
Everyone, it seems, was seeing and hearing it. Everyone,
that is, except Captain Despard, who during the entire
haunting never once saw it. All the Despard sisters constantly heard disembodied footsteps parading through
the house, a cook saw the ghost, and even a neighbor
saw the "weeping woman" out in an orchard in broad
daylight. He, too, mistook it for a living person. In fact,
the ghost was seen almost weekly during the summer of
1885.

However, these phenomena became less and less frequent shortly after. It seemed as though the ghost was
actually "burning itself out," so to speak. Between 1887
and 1889 it appeared only rarely, and it was never seen
at all after that, although it could still be heard sor-
rowfully pacing the staircase and hallways up until 1892.
Miss Despard also noted that the phantom became
much more ghostlike as its appearances became less
common. It often seemed unreal and its legs often sort
of "faded out" as they reached down to the floor. However, even if the Despards could no longer see the figure,
their dog certainly still reacted to it and sometimes became very frightened when the ghost was on the prowl.

Who was this ghost and why did it haunt the
Despards' Cheltenham home? This is a question the
Despards could never answer for sure. Eventually,
though, some old photographs came to light, and Rose
discovered that the apparition closely resembled a picture of Imogene Swinhoe's sister. Since, according to
some longtime residents of the area, the two ladies allegedly looked somewhat alike, Rose concluded that the
ghost was probably that of the former mistress of the
house, even though she hadn't actually died there.

Perhaps her spirit had been drawn back to the house after her death. Or perhaps all the sorrow and emotional agony she had gone through during her years there had left a permanent record on the house . . . a record that somehow the Despards, by their very presence, had activated.

The Cheltenham case can tell us a great deal about the nature of haunted houses. To begin with, it illustrates the fact that haunting phenomena can be physically real, but unreal at the same time. Remember, this ghost could even turn doorknobs! Yet, it remained so phantasmal that it could vanish into thin air or pass right through strings placed in its way. The case is also interesting because the ghost often behaved quite intelligently. For instance, it often deliberately tried to run away from Miss Despard as she tried to corner or speak to it, and would sometimes stare right back at her. In other words, the ghost seemed to know or sense that it was being watched. This ghost was obviously no empty-headed puppet.

But why could Rose see it on some occasions, while no one else in the room could? And why did she see it more often than anyone else? Your guesses are as good as mine, but here are some possibilities:

Could it be that in some mysterious way Rose gave strength to the ghost so that they were somehow psychically bonded together? Could the apparition have drawn some sort of power from the girl? This is a possibility, for Rose herself admits in her notes that when she saw the phantom, she "felt . . . a feeling of loss, as if I had lost power to the figure." Perhaps, too, she was very sensitive to psychic influences and was just more "in tune" with the ghost than was anyone else in the house. On the other hand, perhaps the ghost had deliberately singled Rose out in the hope of making contact with the living. As I suggested in the last chapter, it often seems as if ghosts have the power to appear only to those of their own choosing.

Another puzzling aspect of the Cheltenham haunting is the way in which it simply died out after only a few years of activity. This is unlike most hauntings, which go on for years and years. I certainly can't offer any positive solution to this mystery. However, one theory might be that the ghost was not really the spirit of Imogene Swinhoe at all. Perhaps it was just a three-dimensional picture show about the woman which had somehow been psychically impressed on the house. Then, over the years, perhaps these "psychic pictures" merely faded out just as a piece of film will fade after being constantly replayed. Or maybe Mrs. Swinhoe had somehow "infected" the house with her presence—a living presence which actually survived her physical death and became tied to the house before dissipating. All this may strike you as something out of a *Star Trek* episode or a *Twilight Zone* plot; but then, who is to say what mysterious forces and energies pervade our planet?

Miss Despard was not a very experienced ghost-hunter, although she was undoubtedly a very talented one. A more experienced investigator might have handled the case somewhat differently. And just such an investigator was on hand when, in the 1920s, news about a really wild haunting started hitting the presses.

Borley Church is a twelfth-century structure located some sixty miles out of London, England, and, until its tragic destruction in 1939, a huge house called Borley Rectory was located right across the street. This imposing building has been called "the most haunted house in England." To be sure, it even looked haunted. It was a very large two-story red-brick structure complete with thirty rooms, cellars, corridors, and it even had a few windows crossed with menacing metal bars. The house looked more like a prison than a mansion.

The rectory was built around 1860 by the Reverend Henry Bull, the rector of Borley Church, who lived there until his death in 1892. His son succeeded him as rector of Borley Church and lived in the house until 1927. The next tenants were the Reverend G. Eric Smith and his wife . . . but they moved out the next year. The house was haunted, they said, and they weren't about to stay there any longer than necessary. According to their testimony, they could hear whispering voices at night, and sometimes they would also hear a woman's voice pleading or crying. They saw a shadowy figure stalking the house on more than one occasion, and they saw a phantom nun there as well.

The Smiths, though, were not the only tenants who had encountered this apparition at the Rectory. This same phantom nun had been seen by dozens of people between 1900 and 1927, and it continued to appear up until the year the house was destroyed.

There was quite a tradition about this ghost. In the thirteenth century, according to legend, Borley Church was neighbored by a monastery. A convent also allegedly existed in a town close by. One day, so the story goes, one of the monks eloped with a nun from the convent. Alas, they were caught trying to make their escape. Breaking one's sacred vows was considered the worst sin a monk or nun could commit back in those times, so the would-be lovers were horribly punished. The monk was beheaded while the nun was bricked up alive in a wall of either the church or convent.

This story is, however, only a legend, and there is no evidence that it ever really happened. In fact, no one has ever found any records which would indicate that a monastery or convent even existed anywhere near Borley Church.

Nonetheless, one cannot dismiss the fact that a phantom nun was often seen at the Rectory. It was once collectively witnessed in 1900 by four of Reverend Bull's daughters. They saw the ghost outside the house praying, and one of the girls thought that "there was an expression of intense grief " on the nun's face. The ghost was also seen in 1927 by a handyman who had come to the Rectory to make some repairs. However, a thorough investigation of the Rectory was only made some years later. And what a story it made!

It all started in June, 1929, when the London *Daily Mirror* ran a long story on the haunting of Borley Rectory. This news item came to the attention of Harry Price, one of England's leading authorities on haunted houses. Price was so impressed by the story that he decided to personally visit and investigate the case. Anytime Price got involved in a case, things usually started jumping. His plan was to cross-examine the witnesses and, hopefully, experience some of the ghostly disturbances himself. He wasn't disappointed.

After arriving at the house one day and talking to the occupants, Price explains in one of his two books on the case, he and a reporter from the *Mirror* held watch outside the house from the grounds where the phantom nun had often been seen in the past. Their vigil paid off. After a long wait, the reporter suddenly shouted that he saw a ghostly figure walking up a pathway. Price also thought he saw it, but wasn't sure. So the two investigators ran into the house, but were stopped dead in their tracks when a brick suddenly came crashing through the roof and landed at their feet! But that wasn't the only surprise the ghost-hunters were in for. As they walked down the hallway and away from the downstairs stairwell, they encountered even more psychic surprises. Price recounts them in his book *The End of Borley Rectory*:

As we reached the hall again a red-glass candlestick hurtled down the well of the Rectory and smashed at our feet. We ran upstairs . . . and found that the ornament was one of a pair normally reposing on the mantelpiece of the Blue Room, one of the bedrooms in which many phenomena occurred. We again searched the place from top to bottom, but found no sign of a living thing. Then we were pelted with mothballs, pebbles, bits of slate, etc. All these missiles came from the upper storey . . . Later several of the bells rang of their own volition, and we could actually see the pulls moving, though not what was pulling them!*

In October, 1930, the Reverend L.A. Foyster, his wife, and their twelve-and-a-half-year-old daughter became the new residents of Borley Rectory. It wasn't long, though, before they too realized that they were stuck in a haunted house. Luckily, they kept Price informed about all the eerie events they witnessed.

As the months rolled by, the Foysters continually encountered a startling array of psychic phenomena. Sometimes the mansion became downright frightening. The household bells often rang by themselves, odd odors would sometimes drive the Foysters nearly frantic and—perhaps most amazing of all—handwriting would appear scribbled on the Rectory walls as though some ghost were trying to make contact with the living. These notes, which were more often than not addressed to the Foysters' daughter, often asked for help, but the writer never quite made it known what kind of "help" it wanted. On other occasions the ghost would become nasty, and Mrs. Foyster was sometimes hit in the face by an invisible foe. Once she was struck so hard she began to bleed under the eye. In an attempt to stop the haunting, Reverend Foyster held an exorcism in the house, but the ritual did little good. Mrs. Foyster saw a fright-

---

*Most old English families who lived in large homes had servants who lived with them. Bells were usually hooked in their rooms and wires from them led to most rooms in the house and usually ran across the ceilings. Each room had one or two "bell cords" or "pulls" which were long pieces of material directly attached to the overhead wires. When a servant was needed, the master or mistress of the house merely had to pull the cord up and down. This jiggled the wires which, in turn, rang the bells in the servants' quarters.

ful apparition the very next day.

Because of all the wonders the Foysters had witnessed
at Borley Rectory, Price decided to renew his personal
investigation. He felt, though, that Mrs. Foyster might
have been faking some of the psychokinesis (PK)
herself. However, in 1935 the Foysters moved out and,
after two years during which the house was left unoccupied, Price rented the Rectory himself. This time,
though, he decided to step up his investigation. He collected together forty-eight people to help him, and with
their assistance he was able to keep the house under constant guard day and night for a period of one year. Each
person kept a record of anything odd which he or she
experienced in the house.

Price's plan apparently worked very well. As he wrote
in one of his books on this strange case:

> I will say at once that most of the major
> phenomena were experienced under scientific condi-
> tions. The nun was seen again: many footsteps and
> similar sounds were heard; raps, taps and knockings
> were frequent; there were many para-normal move-
> ments of objects, and appearances, disappearances
> and reappearances of strange articles; a luminous
> phenomenon, pleasant and unpleasant odours, sensa-
> tion of coldness, tactual phenomena, etc.

One of Price's witnesses was even able to watch the
bizarre pencil messages, which had so often been found
etched on the Rectory walls, actually appear before his
very eyes:

> On another occasion Mr. Mark Kerr-Pearse (a
> British pro-consul at Geneva) was alone in the Rec-
> tory and was having his evening meal in the Base
> Room with the door closed. He heard the key in the
> lock turn. Something had locked him in. The ex-

traordinary thing was that the key was on the inside of the door. Consequently whatever locked him in remained in the room ... On May 8, 1938, Mr. M. Savage, a B.B.C. television engineer, and a friend named Bowden reported new pencillings which 'appeared' *while they actually watched the walls.*

Price's lease ran out in May, 1938, so the investigation came to an end at that time. Only a few months later, on February 27, 1939, an oil lamp fell over by itself and sent the Rectory up in flames. But ghosts may be well immune to fire. At least three witnesses who watched the Rectory burn down thought they saw apparitions walking amongst the flames. A month later, a phantom figure was even seen among the ruins.

Price eventually collected all his notes and records concerning the house and wrote two thick books on the case, *The Most Haunted House in England,* and *The End of Borley Rectory.* If you ever want to read a truly fantastic and disturbing "ghost-story," these are the books for you!

The Cheltenham haunting and the restless ghosts of Borley Rectory are two of the most famous haunted houses ever recorded and investigated. Yet they are very similar to the types of hauntings which have been reported only recently. Every year, it seems, more and more hauntings are reported to parapsychology organizations and clubs all over the country. Few of these, though, are ever properly investigated, and many of them, upon investigation, turn out to be nothing but hoaxes.

Many other haunted houses which hit the news, or which are reported to psychical research groups, turn out to be due to very natural causes. The first haunting I ever investigated was back in 1967. A man claimed that loud knockings were keeping him awake at night and he was sure a ghost was loose in his house. He wasn't lying about the noises at all. But it turned out, when I investigated the case personally, that his gas heater was malfunctioning and was kicking up quite a racket. Only shortly after, I got wind of another haunted house. This family complained to me that ghostly footsteps and tappings were heard in their home nightly. Some leaky pipes under the floor were the cause of this one.

Cases such as these can teach us a valuable lesson: despite what you may read, hauntings are not common occurrences. They don't grow on trees. Many people seem to think that they are continually cropping up all over the place, just waiting to be investigated. This is hardly the case, and for every real haunting you might encounter, ten or twenty others will turn out to be fakes. And believe me, you meet a lot of nuts and very sick people in this business, too. Nonetheless, *real* hauntings do crop up now and then, and these cases are what makes ghost-hunting so thrilling.

One of the most peculiar cases which has come to light over the last few years concerns not a haunted house, but a haunted duplex in Pittsburgh, Pennsylvania. (A duplex is a double house, with two apartments, one alongside or atop the other, like a tiny apartment building.) The case was originally investigated by Henry W. Pierce, a science writer for the Pittsburgh *Post-Gazette,* who was not only able to interview all the witnesses, but also to dig deep into the history of the house. The house itself was not an old one. Quite the contrary, it was only three years old when the haunting took hold in the summer of 1971. It was a two-story house, with a staircase inside which led to the upstairs residence.

Mr. and Mrs. Ellsworth Cramer lived upstairs and were the principle witnesses to the haunting. They were a couple with a newborn baby, and young Cramer worked as an engineer at a local steel company. Mrs. Cramer is a registered nurse. As they explained to Pierce, even before they moved into the house they knew something was wrong. Everytime they came to clean it up while they were preparing to move in, they would find the living room light turned on. This happened over and over again, no matter how carefully they turned it off before leaving. The same thing started to happen again several months after they actually moved in. What was even more unnerving, Mrs. Cramer's radio would turn on by itself.

It was not until February, 1972, though, that Mrs. Cramer first started seeing a ghost in the apartment. She always seemed to get a glance of it hovering in the dining area as she walked from her bedroom to the bathroom late at night. At first the apparition didn't appear very humanlike, but looked more like a white cloud. Soon after, Mrs. Cramer started hearing strange noises from the *downstairs* apartment, as if cupboards were being opened and closed, even when nobody was home. And as if this wasn't enough, one day a pair of salt and pepper shakers hurled themselves at the frightened young wife as she walked through the kitchen, and they landed at her feet.

"I was so scared," she told Pierce, "because I thought whatever was doing these things might hurt the baby . . . this was the first time any[thing] seemed directed at a person in an angry sort of way."

Mrs. Cramer had good cause to be frightened. The very same week that she encountered the flying salt and pepper shakers, she saw a dark, shadowy form darting about her baby's room. She was so scared by the ghost that she snatched up the infant and ran downstairs to stay with her neighbor. But the manifestation wasn't over by any means. Even though her apartment was now totally empty, both Mrs. Cramer and her neighbor could hear strange noises coming from it. It sounded as though someone was upstairs moving the furniture all about. Two hours later, Mrs. Cramer built up enough courage to return to her own apartment; there she found her kitchen chairs scattered about the room as though someone had been playing with them.

The climax to the case came a week later when one night both Mr. and Mrs. Cramer heard the voice of a child laughing. Mrs. Cramer heard it first.

"I was shocked to hear it," she explained. "It seemed to come from in the baby's crib, almost as if it was coming from in her or through her."

But Mrs. Cramer could see quite plainly that her little daughter wasn't laughing. The laughter was apparently quite loud and distinct, since it woke her husband who was sleeping in the next room.

Mr. Cramer wasn't too surprised by the laughter, though. He had become well aware that there was something spooky about the apartment. He also had seen some sort of shadow-apparition previously and had watched it float right through their bedroom door.

All during the time the Cramers were going through their nightmare, Mr. and Mrs. Peter Henry, who lived downstairs, were having their troubles too. They were a young couple also, and had moved into the house with their two young sons in July, 1971. They often found lights turned on in their apartment after they had turned them off, just as the Cramers had. Mrs. Henry also admitted to Pierce that she had heard strange footsteps parading around her apartment on several occasions and had once seen a misty sort of apparition. Interestingly enough, she had once heard the disembodied laughter of a child in *her* apartment. Mr. Henry was not immune to the ghost either. Several months before his wife suspected that they were playing host to a ghost, he had encountered a phantom at the top of the staircase leading to the Cramer's apartment. The phantom was only a shadowy figure and he didn't quite know what to make of it.

"I looked again," he told Pierce, "and saw it was not a shadow. It had depth. It was three-dimensional. It moved . . . across the landing . . . and disappeared. I went up to the landing and looked around the corner and there was no one there."

Henry Pierce, who carried out several interviews with the concerned families, became so interested in the case that he tried to track down the history of the house. Could some terrible death have occurred there, he wondered? Possibly that of a child? But by checking police records, the investigator learned that no such deaths had ever occurred in the building. However, he did discover one odd thing. One of the previous tenants had once had a nine-year-old son who was very disturbed. He had lived a good part of his life in a mental institution. One day he fell from a window and was killed. The grief-stricken woman had moved into the duplex shortly after the accident.

Could the ghost of the boy have followed his mother to her new home? This is one possible solution to the mystery, and even Pierce concludes his report on the case by stating that the boy's "personality, his death by violence, his association . . . with the house in question . . . all lend support to the hypothesis that it was he, rather than any living person, who served as agent for the reported phenomena."

Is there any sure-fire way to tell if a house is genuinely haunted? This is one problem the psychical investigator faces whenever he gets called into a case. Parapsychologists must act like detectives. We haven't witnessed the events in question ourselves, so all we can do is collect all the evidence, reconstruct the events and then cross-examine the witnesses once more about the things they saw or *thought* they saw or heard. This is a very difficult job, though, since people who believe or claim that they live in haunted houses will sometimes exaggerate their stories, tell lies about their experiences, or will often very honestly misinterpret perfectly normal noises, creaks, shadows, or light reflections. (You would be surprised to learn just how many "ghosts" turn out to be reflections from automobile lights!) Because of these difficulties, a few parapsychologists have recently tried to explore haunted houses by using new and more interesting techniques. One such investigation was made in 1966 right in my home town of Los Angeles.

As I've said over and over again, any house might become haunted. Even famous Hollywood personalities, who live in luxurious modern homes, sometimes get stuck with a ghost. And that's just what happened to Elke Sommers, the beautiful Swedish actress, when in 1964 several visitors to her elegant Benedict Canyon home started seeing a mysterious man wearing a white shirt walking about both inside the house and in the backyard. During the same time, Elke Sommers and her husband, Joe Hyams, started hearing strange sounds in the house at night, such as phantom footsteps and other ghostly noises.

Rather unnerved by the whole affair, the Hyams contacted the University of California at Los Angeles in the hope that they might have a resident ghost-hunter who could help them out and solve the mystery. The case was turned over to two psychiatrists and they, in turn, asked the cooperation of the Los Angeles branch of the American Society for Psychical Research in making an investigation. A special A.S.P.R. team was organized to look into the case and Dr. Thelma Moss, a psychologist from U.C.L.A. was put in charge. Dr. Moss decided to do more than just collect all the testimony on the case. She wanted to see if they could learn a little about the nature of the ghost.

To carry out her plan, Dr. Moss and her team asked six people who seemed to possess psychic ability to visit the house when no one was home. Each was given a floor plan of the house and was told to mark off any place where they felt that the ghost's presence was particularly strong or active. They were also given a list of words which could possibly describe the ghost, such as "friendly," "harmful," "menacing," and so on. Each psychic was asked to go through the list and try to determine which adjectives applied to the ghost, and which did not. Another list was given to them which consisted of words that might describe the physical appearance of the ghost. Of course, each psychic visited the house independently. Eight other people *without* psychic ability also visited the house and carried out the same tests.

When all the results were compiled, the A.S.P.R. investigators discovered that three of the psychics agreed remarkably well on the nature and appearance of the ghost. Their impressions also agreed with information and descriptions which Hyams and Miss Sommers had given to the investigators. So these psychics may well have actually been "picking up" something from or about the ghost. For instance, they tended to pick up the impression that the ghost was a slightly elderly man, but that he was not out to cause any real trouble. One psychic correctly ascertained that the dining room was the "seat" of the haunting. (This bit of information tallied with Elke Sommers's claim that the nightly noises she had so often heard seemed to come primarily from the kitchen and dining areas of the house.) On the other hand, there was no agreement at all about the haunting among the eight non-psychic people who also visited the house.

However, a couple of the psychics did feel that the house was being haunted by a menacing presence. Perhaps the most disturbing impression about the haunting was received by Jacqueline Eastlund, a well-known local psychic, who visited the house several times and who eventually became a good friend of the Hyams'.

"I see your dining room in flames next year; be careful," she warned her hosts during one of her visits.

All this did little to ease the situation, though. Even with the U.C.L.A. professors studying the house and with psychics galore tramping about, the Hyams were still stuck with their ghost. Hyams checked with previous owners of the house and learned that they, too, had experienced strange phenomena there. The ghost was there to stay, or so it seemed. So in the spring of 1967 the Hyams just plain got fed up with the whole thing and decided to move out. The next day a mysterious fire broke out in the dining room and severely damaged the house.

Jacqueline Eastlund's prediction had come true!

Unfortunately, using psychics to help investigate a haunted house is really not a very good way of handling a case. Take Dr. Moss's investigation for instance. One could argue that the A.S.P.R. psychics were just tuning in to each other by telepathy. So their impressions about the ghost might not have been related to the haunting at all. They might also have been picking up information directly from the minds of Joe Hyams or Miss Sommers. So, bringing a psychic or two into a haunted house may not be of much help as you try to discover the cause of a haunting. To be sure, a psychic brought in to investigate a haunted house might come up with some interesting information, but you can never be sure whether or not this information is really correct. For example, one psychic who visited the Hyams's house felt that the ghost was of a European man who had never lived in the house at all. But how are we, as investigators, supposed to check out a piece of information such as this?

A very different approach to the study of hauntings is currently being made by the Durham, North Carolina-based Psychical Research Foundation. The P.R.F. is one of the few full-time parapsychology labs in the United States and is headquartered in a small three-building complex in one of the prettiest tree-studded parts of Durham. It was founded in 1960 by Charles E. Ozanne, a wealthy college teacher, for one special purpose. It was specifically endowed to study those psychic phenomena which indicate that man might survive death. W.G. Roll, an Oxford-educated parapsychologist, became project director for the organization and is still the guid-

ing light behind its work. Since the P.R.F. is located
right next to Duke University, Roll has been fortunate
enough to recruit several scientists from the college to
help the Foundation in its attempt to explore psychic
phenomena. Among these scientists have been electrical
engineers, psychologists, physicists, and even biologists.

Over the past seventeen years, Roll and his group
have been especially interested in investigating reports
of haunted houses. When a promising case is reported to
them or hits the press, Roll will usually send out a team
of researchers right to the spot as soon as possible. Their
job is to gather up all the evidence they can about the
haunting, stay in the house if possible, and carry out
sometimes delicate experiments in order to detect any
odd energies or forces which might be present.

The following report is a summary of a typical P.R.F.
investigation. It was made in 1968 by Dr. William T.
Joines, who is an assistant professor of electrical engi-
neering at Duke, as well as one of the P.R.F.'s leading
investigators. For this case, the P.R.F. sent Dr. Joines to
Norfolk, Virginia, where two families were complaining
that their apartment building was haunted. Although a
bit technical, this short report will give you a rough idea
as to how a modern parapsychologist goes about his job:

The reported disturbances occurred in the apartments of Mr. and Mrs. W.W. Franks and Mr. and
Mrs. Paul Ruby. The Franks have five children ages
seven to three, and the Rubys have two, ages about
four and three. The Franks occupied an upstairs
apartment and the Rubys the downstairs apartment
directly underneath in an eight-unit apartment building. Mr. Franks and Mr. Ruby are naval enlistees,
both about thirty years of age. The disturbances
which were said to have started toward the end of
August, 1967, continued until January, 1968, at
which time Franks and Ruby received new location
assignments from the Navy.

Among the incidents described by the Franks were the movement of furniture and tearing of clothing and paper money, the sound of a baby crying, knocks, footsteps, cold spots within rooms, a broken window, and a cuckoo clock that fell from the wall and landed on the floor about eight feet from the wall. The disturbances mentioned by the Rubys were less intense and less frequent. These included cold spots, rattling sounds in the kitchen and the movement of kitchen utensils.

In response to a phone call to Mr. W.G. Roll from Mr. Jack Kestner, a reporter at the Norfolk *Ledger-Star,* and to reports from Franks, the case was first investigated November 10–12, 1967. Mr. John Stump, a psychology student at the University of North Carolina at Chapel Hill, collaborated in the study. The investigators brought a tape recorder, a camera, and three thermistor-type temperature measuring instruments.* During the two days and nights of this investigation no cold spots were detected by the instruments, even in the areas where Mrs. Ruby claimed she felt them. No unusual sounds or movements were observed or detected during the daylight hours. However, both nights, with all adults in the Ruby's downstairs apartment, unusual sounds from the upstairs apartment were heard by both investigators as well as by the Rubys and Franks. The noises, which were not attributed to the children, sounded like furniture being moved, an object rolling or tumbling across the floor, and a heavy creaking and thumping of the floor. During the time of these occurrences, the tape recorder was left on in the upstairs apartment and the investigators wrote down a description of each sound and the time to the nearest second, so that the written record could be compared

---

*These are very delicate thermometers which can detect very tiny changes in temperature.

with the tape recording. Reasonably good correlation between these two records was obtained during both nights, and some of the sounds still lack an acceptable explanation.

The P.R.F. investigates several such cases a year. In 1973, for instance, they learned about a haunted house in New Brunswick, New Jersey. The two-story house, in which one family and three renters lived, had quite a legend attached to it. The house was only fifty years old, and the original owner had been killed in a train accident in 1937. The people who were presently living in the house had come to believe that his body was buried underneath the house. This notion, like so many legends that become attached to haunted houses, was proved wrong upon subsequent investigation. The body had lain in a nearby cemetery for years! Nonetheless, in 1972 the house started playing games with the tenants. A hall lamp would swing by itself, doors would unlock, and good old-fashioned mysterious footsteps stomped up and down the staircase. So in May, the P.R.F. sent out one of their investigators, Robert Rosenberg, to look into the case.

Rosenberg's visit was certainly exciting enough. He was mainly interested in the family's claim that the hallway lighting fixture would often be found swinging to and fro. Naturally, he checked to see if any air currents might be present inside the house which could account for these movements. Despite his search, Rosenberg could find no normal cause for the phenomenon. Later on during the day he was personally able to watch—and photograph—the lamp swinging by itself.

As the day rolled on, Rosenberg also discovered that "some one" had placed a cuckoo clock in his camera case when he wasn't looking. It had apparently "teleported" (see glossary) there all by itself. He removed it of course, but the exact same thing happened again later on during his stay at the house. On another occasion, Rosenberg found a knife under the latch of the case, which had apparently been mysteriously placed there when he was investigating another part of the house.

A very different kind of haunting was reported to the P.R.F. in February, 1974. This one was located in Salisbury, Maryland, and it sounded much like a conventional ghost story. This house was also a two-story one and was occupied by a middle-aged couple (called Mr. and Mrs. C. in the report), their three children, and a family friend.* No one ever actually saw a ghost in the house, but all the residents swore to investigators that they had heard footsteps and other peculiar sounds coming from the staircase when it was obvious that no one was there. They had heard these noises ever since they first moved in. They also claimed that the doorbell chimes often rang by themselves.

After receiving an initial report on the case, the P.R.F. sent William Eisler to look into the matter. Eisler was very impressed by the family's testimony and reported to the P.R.F.:

> The most frequently reported disturbance was the sound of footsteps, which seven people report having heard on at least one occasion. What is usually heard is the sound of someone walking up the stairs and/or along the upstairs hall. All accounts agree that the steps are at a normal-to-slow pace and of moderate loudness (i.e. not heavy). The sounds do not seem like

---

*In many cases, people who find themselves trapped in a haunted house don't want publicity. They just want relief. So in many reports investigators will not use the real names of the people involved. This protects their privacy. Their true names, though, are usually filed with the organization in charge of the investigation, so that the identities of the witnesses are always on hand and available to qualified parapsychologists.

creaks in the woodwork. Included among the seven witnesses are two visitors, both of whom characterized themselves as skeptics with regard to parapsychological phenomena. Mrs. C.'s sister, Adelaide, age 20, told me that one night when she was babysitting for the three younger children she heard footsteps over the living room. It struck her as unusual because all four of them were downstairs watching television, and to her knowledge no one had entered the house.

Sometimes the footsteps were collectively heard on other occasions as well. Mrs. C. told Eisler that both she and her husband had heard them in an overhead room while they were watching T.V. late in the evening. All the children in the house were accounted for at the time. Mrs. C. also claimed that she had discovered small "cold spots"—which are often felt in haunted places—in the house. Unfortunately, Eisler failed to detect any of these himself.

So what does all this mean? This is a hard question to answer. However, these fascinating cases do point out a few basic things about haunted houses. First, they prove that haunted houses are just as active today as they have been in the past. Also, you can see that some very well-educated people and scientists are doing their best to explore these places. People who believe that only the superstitious or the gullible believe in ghosts and haunted houses just don't know what they are talking about!

These cases also offer some good tips to any potential ghost-hunter who might be reading this book. Note how important it is to take down all the testimony about a haunting, talk with all the witnesses available to you, and compare their stories. If the house is genuinely haunted, there should be some general agreement among all the reports as to what has been going on. Also, you must check out the history of any house you investigate. There, hidden in some old records, may be the information which will help you discover why the house is haunted and who the "haunter" might be. Ghost-hunting is not an easy job by any means, and it is a subject which will be discussed at greater length later.

3. A DIARY OF A HAUNTED HOUSE

What's it like to actually live in an honest-to-goodness haunted house?

I guess everyone who is interested in psychic phenomena has asked himself this question. I know I have. And I know that most of my fellow ghost-hunters have too. After all, it's only natural. After reading about hauntings and investigating case after case, you actually begin to envy the people you've met who have personally lived in these strange places. However, it wasn't until after I had been chasing ghosts for a long time that I was able to move into a haunted house myself. That's when I found out what life in a haunted house is *really* like. It's an adventure of a lifetime.

If I were to show you the haunted house in which I lived for two years, I doubt if you would notice anything unusual about it. It certainly doesn't look like the type of haunted house you so often see portrayed in the movies. It isn't run-down, no bats circle about the attic, and there aren't any hidden passageways inside. Passers-by don't hear ghastly shrieks coming from the house, and no one has ever seen a sheet-clad ghost lurking behind its windows.

Instead, it is an old-fashioned 1920-ish little Spanish-style house which sits in the middle of a block alongside other similar houses. The street is in a quiet, tree-lined suburb, and the house looks just like any other you might see in any old Los Angeles neighborhood. Inside, it has two small bedrooms, one at the front of the house adjoining the living room, and one at the rear. The living room opens into a large den, right smack in the middle of the house, which leads into the back bedroom. The house is pretty plain and stark. But for some reason it harbors an eerie force which I spent two years confronting and trying to understand.

I first learned about the house in 1971 when two friends of mine, Dennis and Carlos, moved in. They were both ex-college buddies of mine. In fact, during our college days we had all once shared an apartment together, so I knew them rather well. At least I knew them well enough to know that they weren't superstitious or prone to practical joking. Carlos, who had only recently moved to Los Angeles from San Diego, was only twenty-one at the time and was studying to become a concert violinist. Dennis was also a musician, but surfing was his real major love in life. He was a bit older than Carlos, and only lived in the house for about six months before moving away from Los Angeles permanently. Both of them knew of my interest in ghost-hunting, of course, but had little idea that my interest and knowledge would eventually focus right in on the house in which they lived.

Carlos and Dennis moved into the house in January. At first the two of them didn't realize that they were living in a haunted house. Everything just seemed so normal then. I used to visit them every so often. And believe me, ghosts were not exactly a common topic of conversation. However, after several months Dennis and Carlos began to realize that there was something strange going on in their home.

"You know, there's something odd about this place," Carlos told me one day in the summer of 1971.

"What do you mean," I asked, not at first realizing what my friend was getting at.

"Well," Carlos continued, "it all started when we opened up the chimney flue. Ever since then strange things have been happening in the house."

Carlos went on to tell me that it seemed like a spook

had been liberated in the house when the chimney was opened. Household items suddenly started to disappear mysteriously, never to be seen again; records would vanish from his collection only to reappear out of order later on; and when he returned home from work he would find things moved about as though someone had been in the house while he was gone. He even claimed that once he found his two pet dogs inside the house when he *knew* he had left them outside!

Carlos wasn't the only person I spoke to who knew that the house harbored some supernatural secret. Dennis, for instance, had also felt the presence of the "force" in the house.

"Everything was just fine," the tall, twenty-two-year-old blond surfer told me, "until we opened the flue in the chimney. It was like some force was let loose in the house. It's weird."

I was also able to talk to two other people who had had strange experiences in the house. One of them had been so freaked out by what happened that he didn't want to talk about it at all. "Weird things go on here," was just about the only thing he would tell me. However, he did say that some of his possessions had mysteriously vanished one time while staying at the house. Another witness told me how a vacuum cleaner had mysteriously turned itself on one night when no one was near it. And this guest didn't even know that the house was supposed to be haunted.

All in all, the case sounded promising. Just think, the house was only a few miles from where I lived and seemed to have a ghost lurking about just waiting for me to investigate . . . a ghost which made itself known by stealing things, moving household objects about, and turning on vacuum cleaners. Whatever the force was, it seemed to be trying to call attention to itself. And it was doing a pretty good job of it. In fact, maybe too good. I can recall that on several occasions Carlos suggested to me that he was ready to move out. A ghost just wasn't his idea of an ideal roommate. So, starting in 1971 I began to visit the house often to keep close tabs on anything unusual that might go on there. I must have visited the house dozens of times, often staying until late in the night, but I never saw or heard anything strange or mystifying. In fact, I began to doubt if the house actually was haunted. I was soon to learn differently.

In December, 1971 I got the chance of a lifetime. Carlos was living alone at the time and offered to rent me the back bedroom. The idea appealed to me since I was sick of my apartment, was just about to finish up my college work, and wanted to move into a house. The chance to move into a haunted one was an opportunity I just couldn't resist. So, in January of 1972 I moved into the house and lived there until the January of 1974, during which time I had many ghostly encounters.

On the night of April 16th, I was out for the evening and Carlos was studying some music in his bedroom when the first eerie events took place. The only other occupant in the house was our Great Dane, a beautiful and gentle female named Duchess, who was very busy chewing a bone when the ghost made its presence known that night.

As Carlos told me in the morning, he was lying on his bed when he suddenly heard the screen door open and shut, and the front door open and then slam close. He merely thought I had come home. But then he heard some peculiar sounds. "Thump . . . thump . . . thump," they went. It sounded as though someone were walking heavily across the carpetless living room floor. Again, he merely thought that I had come home. But then Duchess flew into action. With a viciousness totally alien to her nature, she started barking furiously. She lost all interest in her bone and the muscles on her back tightened. Carlos now knew something strange was going on since the dog never barked when I came home, and, in fact, rarely barked at all. To be sure, she was a complete failure as a watchdog. Carlos flew into the living room, thinking that a burglar had gotten in, but when he got there his heart sank. Nobody was there at all! And there was Duchess still barking and staring at the front door looking at something invisible to any human eye. Carlos checked and found that the front door was still securely locked, so no one could actually have entered the house.

During the time I lived in the house, Duchess become our chief ghost detector, since she seemed very sensitive to the spook. I can remember how, one evening while I was alone with her, she seemed to react strikingly to some invisible presence. It all began when I noticed that she was staring intently into the back bedroom. I watched her closely. Her whole body was tense. Then, she slowly crouched down and approached the bedroom, never moving her eyes from whatever she was looking at. I got up and stood behind her, but the dog seemed totally unaware of me. She was only interested in some invisible "thing" in the bedroom. As odd as it may seem, she looked just like a cat stalking a bird. By this time, Duchess had crouched down almost to her stomach and was still stalking, and slowly and deliberately she crept towards the room. Then, as though some magic spell had been broken, she snapped back to normal. She stopped staring into my bedroom, arose, and trotted away as though nothing had happened. "Oh, if animals could only talk!" I thought to myself. I watched Duchess carefully for the rest of the evening, but she acted perfectly normal.

Apart from being a ghost detector, Duchess also played the key role in a truly frightening adventure I once had in the house. The incident occurred one week when the haunting was particularly active. You see, the haunting would go through periods of activity and inactivity. Usually it would act up for a week or so and then nothing would happen for several months. It seemed as though the ghost had to build up its energy, and then used it all up creating the disturbances. We were right in the middle of one of these outbreaks, and the phenomena seemed to be focusing in the front part of the house. I thought I would be in a better position to witness anything that might happen if I slept in the living room that night. So, I lay down on the sofa, put a blanket over myself, and soon began to doze off.

About an hour later I woke up. I was lying on my side and I felt a peculiar pulling on my blanket as though someone were trying to pull it off. I could feel my stomach twist as an eerie feeling came over me. For a second I thought, "Do I dare look up?" Of course I did. A huge phantom head loomed before me at the bottom of the couch. My heart jumped—and so did I with a loud gasp. But then I realized more clearly what had frightened me. It was only Duchess. She had sneaked into the living room and had decided to sniff my feet! We stared at each other for a few moments, and then she pranced out of the room justifiably pleased with herself for scaring the daylights out of me.

I think it was about this time that I decided Duchess should sleep in the kitchen at night! It also goes to show that even we hard-headed, nerves-of-steel ghost-hunters can get scared too.

But let's get back to the *real* phenomena.

The day after Carlos heard the phantom footsteps, he had another ghostly encounter. He was asleep in his room when he awoke to hear what he described as "humming sounds". They were distinct, he told me, but he couldn't isolate the source of the noise.

By this time the haunting was in its full glory, and I first began to personally confront "the force," or whatever was invading the house. My initial experiences took place at about the same time that Carlos was hearing the phantom footsteps and the humming sounds. My encounters started one afternoon as I was lying on my bed. All of a sudden—"Whack!" It felt like someone had hit the bed with his fist or kicked it, and I could feel the whole bed shake under me. (Incidentally, bed shakings are a typical phenomenon which many people who have lived in haunted houses complain about.)

These bed shakings occurred day after day . . . when I retired at night, before I got up in the morning, and when I tried to take a nap in the afternoon. It seemed as though our ghostly friend was trying to annoy me any time I tried to get a little rest. Sometimes the bed was given such powerful jolts that I could actually hear as well as feel the box springs shake for a couple of seconds.

By this time, the haunting had been going on for five days. I examined the bed completely, pulled it apart and looked over the frame, checked the box springs for a loose spring that might be acting up, and checked over the mattress. I couldn't find anything out of order. So on April 22nd, I decided to see if I could make mental contact with the ghost. As I lay in bed that night I mentally commanded: "If there is some entity present, bounce the bed right now!" My request wasn't answered immediately, but a few minutes later my bed was given a staggering blow. I could actually feel some invisible force slam the bed right next to my pillow. The whole bed shook for a few seconds and actually reeled on its metal frame. I was totally awake at the time and there could be no mistake about what I witnessed. But that wasn't the end of the fun.

Two days later, the haunting really got fancy. Carlos reported to me that he had awakened to hear low moaning voices emanating from the wall next to his bed. These cryings and sobbings only lasted a minute or so, but Carlos was fed up. He told me he wanted to move out of the house. At that time it struck me as odd how two people—Carlos and myself—could have such different reactions to the haunting. To me, living in the haunted house was a dream-come-true. To him, the dream was rapidly decaying into a nightmare. It took me some time to assure Carlos that ghosts don't hurt people or cause any damage. He finally calmed down and I could only wish that *I* had heard the phantom voices.

Although I never heard the moaning sounds which Carlos reported, on one occasion I did hear an independent voice in the house. It was the most dramatic incident which I ever witnessed there. The events leading up to the incident started the night of December 26th. I awoke at 3:20 a.m. It was a perfect night for some ghostly visitation. The wind was bellowing outside and I could hear dried leaves scraping over the wooden planks which made up the roof of my room. At the same time my windows were being scraped ominously by the clawlike branches of a huge and magnificent walnut tree which shades the entire backyard. As I awoke I felt a bit uneasy. It was a feeling I quickly recognized. You see, I had become sensitive to the haunting by now and could "feel" when it was about to act up. The house would feel to me as if it was saturated by a dry, static charge. I could feel this "energy" when I woke up that night. Suddenly, I heard what sounded like the strings of a violin being bowed softly. The sounds were coming from right in my room; they were distinct and impressive. I listened to them for a few moments and then they died away as my attention was once again drawn to the frantic wind outside.

"The house is acting up again," I said to myself as I went back to sleep. I knew that we were going to be in for a week or so of manifestations, and I was prepared for that. But I wasn't ready for the shocker that was in store for me.

The next evening, Carlos was busying himself with housework and I was just lazying around the house when this cozy scene was interrupted by a phone call. It was for Carlos from a girl we both knew. They spoke for a while and then hung up. Carlos repeated a story the girl had told him and then, without saying anything more about the conversation, went into the kitchen to tidy up.

"What else did she have to say?" I called out to Carlos from the den a few moments later.

A gruff male voice, speaking sarcastically and in a loud whisper answered. "Nothing . . . nothing . . . nothing," it said. Each word was spoken clearly but gruffly and in a measured rhythm.

The voice was so sarcastic that at first I thought perhaps Carlos was talking to the dog and wasn't talking to me at all. I couldn't understand why he seemed so nasty and I walked into the kitchen to speak to him. There I got the shock of my life. Carlos wasn't in the kitchen. In fact, he wasn't even in the house! He had been outside in the backyard all the time and hadn't even heard me call to him. Over and over again he denied having heard me call out, or to have uttered a single word. I was very perplexed, but then the bizarre truth struck me like a bullet: my question had been answered by a disembodied voice. Now, it seemed, the ghost was ready to talk to us. Our little haunted house was becoming more interesting by the minute.

By this time I had learned a great deal about our invisible friend, so let me tell you a little about him. I had learned, for instance, that rarely during an outbreak would Carlos and I witness the phantom manifestations on the same night. Instead, the ghost would bother me one night, Carlos the next, and so on. It looked as though the spook took turns with us, trying to get each of our attention separately. The ghost seemed neither good nor evil. It just seemed interested in making us aware of its presence. It didn't seem nasty . . . although it banged my bed, groaned about, and often made a general nuisance of itself. However, apart from the ghost, I tend to think that there was *another* force in the house . . . a nasty, evil power. This force was never very predominant in the house, and, as far as I know, only made its presence known once. But I still shudder when I think about my experience with it.

I had lived in the house for quite some time when I first perceived this new force sometime in 1973. After a year of living there I certainly wasn't bothered by the thought of sleeping in the house. I had retired one night at about one in the morning and was soon asleep. The house was going through one of its dry spells, and I wasn't expecting anything to happen. However, I woke up with a start sometime later, with the intuitive feeling that something horrible was staring at me from the wall next to my bed. The feeling was overpowering and I literally panicked. The only thought in my mind was that I had to escape. In an instant I found myself running out of the room as fast as I could. I was hardly even awake. By the time I reached the den, the feeling of terror left me, and I cautiously reentered the bedroom. Whatever had so frightened me was gone; and I went back to bed.

This experience was no delusion. I felt that I was in the presence of something dreadful and that I had to escape it. I've never had a similar experience before or since, and I hope I never do.

Over the two years that I lived in the house, I frequently witnessed all sorts of other disturbances as well. Although invisible, our guest was certainly noisy. Sometimes at night I would hear loud thumping sounds. I could never locate where the noises came from, but I heard them dozens of times. So did some of our earthly house guests, including at least one who did not know that the house was haunted.

Our ghost also liked to steal things. If you recall, back in 1971 Carlos had complained to me that household items and records would mysteriously vanish, and I witnessed this phenomenon myself several times. Now, nothing exactly vanished in front of my very eyes. Our ghost was no magician. Instead, commonly used household articles were forever just getting "lost." For example, our ghost look delight in stealing linen, and I often had to buy new sheets to make up for the ones which had vanished. I know that cartoon ghosts are supposed to appear with sheets draped over their heads, and if this is truly the case then our ghost must have had quite a wardrobe by the time I moved. On another occasion, some medicine I was taking vanished within hours of my specifically placing it in a safe location.

These disappearances went on for the entire two years I lived in the house, and none of the stolen items ever turned up again.

One of the most peculiar phenonenon I witnessed was nothing physical such as a table floating about or a chain-rattling phantom wandering through the house. In fact, I never actually "saw" any ghost during my stay in the house and have always felt rather cheated about that! However, I could *feel* its presence. As I said earlier, sometimes I could sense when the haunting was about to act up, and how the house felt as if it was charged with some force or static. The atmosphere would feel "dry," that's the only word I can use to describe it, and I would feel apprehensive. I can remember that once I told Carlos, "You know, I feel odd . . . something's going to happen in the house." Carlos looked at me knowingly. "I've felt that way for two days," he said. Indeed, the next day the house acted up again. Gradually, both Carlos and I were somehow able to tune in on the haunting and were becoming more and more sensitive to it by the month.

In 1974 I moved away from the house. It was sold to a new owner, my rent was being raised, and I just felt that it was time for me to move on. Carlos had moved out of the house several months before, and it looked like a special era of my life was about to end. But now I had the time to trace the background of the house. Why was it haunted? How did it become that way? Would it remain so? These were the questions which came to my mind as I prepared to move.

My first job was to trace the history of the house, and by doing some background research into the neighbor-

hood I learned that it had originally been built in the late
1920s. The second bedroom, in which I had lived, had
been added on in the 1950s by subsequent owners. The
house didn't seem to have any history of being haunted.
I even spoke to one couple who had lived in the house
for ten years and they said they never had encountered
anything unusual. I checked with the owners. None of
the previous tenants, they claimed, had ever complained
of any spooky goings-on in the house. Also, I might add,
the haunting affected both the older and the newer parts
of the house. So, perhaps the haunting had only started
recently.

Why was this ordinary, drab-looking little Spanish-
style house haunted? One possible answer came my way
just before the time came for me to move. I was talking
with the owner, who was out at the house to fix the
plumbing. He was a friendly and talkative old guy, and
I decided to pump him for a few details about the
house's early history.

"Do you know who first owned this house?" I asked
him casually.

"Sure," he answered in a second, "it was the Reverend Paris. He lived here for twenty years. Then we
bought the place after his wife died."

Then the owner said something which really got me
interested.

"Did you know that this house used to be a wedding
chapel?" he asked with a hint of pride in his voice.
"Yep," he went on, "hundreds of people got hitched
here."

This was a surprise! It also explained the odd floor
plan of the house. As I pointed out at the beginning of
this chapter, the whole house had been remodeled
around a large den, and you had to go through it to get
to any other room. This den had been the wedding
chapel, and for twenty years the minister and his wife
had conducted marriages here. I subsequently learned
that in the 1940s Mrs. Paris had fallen ill and died in a

local hospital. Her husband had sold the house and moved out shortly after. The present owners had bought the place and had added on the second bedroom.

I can't dismiss the possibility that the fact that the house was formerly a chapel might have something to do with the haunting. Could the strong emotions associated with the ceremonies which had taken place there have created the haunting? Or could the reverend's wife, who spent so many years in the house, still be lingering about? One thing is for sure, though. The fact that the house was a wedding chapel and is now haunted couldn't be merely coincidental. It's just too odd.

But why did Carlos and I experience the haunting, while other tenants did not? Had the force been slowly growing and growing over the years and only first made its presence known in the 1970s?

These are questions which will remain forever unanswered. However, later in this book I'll explain a little about how we *think* a house might become haunted.

I haven't lived in that little haunted house for four years now. I miss it. In fact, I often find myself drawn to it and every once in awhile I'll find myself driving about my old neighborhood. I sometimes just stop across the street and stare at the house. It's been repainted, reroofed, modernized, and it's a much cheerier place now than when I lived there. But I always wonder as I look at it: what is going on there now? Is the haunting still going on? What strange encounters might the new tenants have to report?

Some day, I'll ring the doorbell and find out.

4. EVIL HAUNTINGS

Sometime in the early part of 1903, the *Ivan Vassilli* sailed from Russia to Siberia carrying a cargo of military supplies. The steamer had been built in 1897, so it was a relatively modern ship at the time of the voyage. None of the crew thought much of the cruise, since it was no different than any of the countless others the ship had made. The voyage, its cargo, and its route were all strictly routine.

But then "it" struck.

No one quite knew what "it" was. It seemed to be at one and the same time a force, an energy, a ghost, and a ghoul. But one thing was for sure . . . it was evil. So evil and terrible, in fact, that men killed themselves rather than face it.

The strange story of the ill-fated *Ivan Vassilli* is not fiction. As I pointed out in Chapter 1, the commonly held belief that ghosts are out for vengeance or to do harm to the living is more legend and myth than fact. But I also warned you that there were exceptions to this rule. In this chapter we'll take a look at some of these exceptions . . . and in all their gruesome detail. Hauntings can become awfully bothersome, that's for sure. Some haunted houses, such as the terrible villa of Comeada, Portugal, and Borley Rectory, have been known to punch or slap their tenants around a bit. Many people who have lived in haunted houses have likewise complained that, at times, they were thrown to the floor or punched in the stomach by some quite invisible force. But if some hauntings can get nasty, others sometimes get downright evil. The *Ivan Vassilli* is a good case in point.

The *Ivan Vassilli* had no reputation for being haunted, and between the years 1897 and 1903 she had sailed the seven seas courageously but uneventfully. There was certainly no hint that any ghost—or any other type of supernatural being, for that matter—was lurking about her decks. There was nothing very unique about the ship either. It was only one of many steamers the Russian navy was using at the turn of the century. But her voyage to Siberia in 1903 soon turned into a nightmare for everyone aboard. It was only the first, though, of four terror trips the ship made before she was destroyed.

The horror all began one otherwise calm night when several of the crew suddenly "felt" an evil presence on board ship. No one actually saw anything, but eventually everyone could definitely feel the "ghost's" malicious presence. It felt as though the whole ship were being saturated with evil, and this presence grew so powerful that it became totally overwhelming. Yet, there was absolutely nothing anyone could do about it and no one could isolate the source of the evil. It was just "there," pervading the decks. Panic took over the ship, and finally one of the crew members, a seaman named Alec Govinski, became so horror-stricken that he jumped overboard in order to escape the invisible menace.

Govinski was to be the first of the ghoul's long line of victims. However, at the time, as though his suicide were an unholy sacrifice to some savage god, the seaman's death seemed to satisfy the ghost and its evil presence simply vanished from the ship almost immediately afterwards.

This relief didn't last long, though. Three days later, the "thing," as the crew began to call the force, was back, and once again everyone could feel its very real—but also quite invisible—presence. This time, however, the force didn't seem as strong, and luckily the *Ivan*

Vassilli reached port the next day. Had it not, no doubt the crew would have mutinied or abandoned ship. As it was, several sailors tried to desert after the ship docked, but, unfortunately for them, they were all recaptured and the ship set sail for Hong Kong the next day.

Like the Siberian trip, this voyage soon became a horror. As the *Ivan Vassilli* slowly made its way south, the crew could feel the evil presence aboard ship once again, growing and growing in power just as it had during their last cruise. Whatever the vile thing was, it was obviously making the ship its permanent home. And, as it grew in strength, it even began to take on human form. A few of the crew actually saw the ghost and claimed that it was a misty form vaguely resembling a human being. However, even though the ghost was now becoming visible to them, the crew once again reacted to it with sheer, naked panic. It seemed that the men were not so much reacting to the apparition itself, but rather to the sense of unbearable evil which the creature always carried with it whether it became visible or not. By the time the trip was over, two seamen had deliberately taken their own lives and a third literally died of fright as they tried to escape from the ship. Even the captain, Sven Andrist, jumped overboard after coming into contact with the "force," and the rest of the crew deserted the vessel as soon as it reached port.

This is certainly a ghastly story. But is it really true, or is it merely a bit of rather effective fiction?

This is a hard question to answer. Indeed, you might find the *Vassilli* affair a little hard to believe. The case does read more like a good old-fashioned ghost story than a well-documented haunting. That's certainly how the case struck me when I first read about it some ten years ago. However, I began reconsidering it in 1973 after I had my own brief encounter with psychic evil in my own home. That was a truly frightening experience and, in light of it, I can well believe that anyone who might be so unfortunate as to encounter this type of evil more than once might well be driven to suicide in order to escape from it. If you will recall, I also literally panicked for a moment in the face of this power and found myself —almost involuntarily—running from my room in sheer fright. Could these men have been reacting the same way I did, but on an even more desperate scale? This strikes me as very possible. For them, though, the only escape was the open sea.

The *Ivan Vassilli* made only two more trips during her brief career; one to Australia and another to San Francisco. In each case, foreign crews had to be hired to sail her, since no Russian sailor would so much as set foot aboard her. However, on both these trips the "thing" constantly stalked the vessel and both voyages were filled with tragedy as seaman after seaman—and captain after captain—either killed themselves or jumped overboard whenever the "thing" began to walk about. One captain became so horrified by the evil that he shot himself through the head while in a state of complete panic.

But what was the "thing" looking for? Was it actually hunting down human victims? Was it conscious of its destructive acts? No one—that is, no one who sailed aboard the ship and lived—could ever come up with any answers to these questions.

The only clue we have about the nature of the *Vassilli* horror comes to us from Harry Nelson, a one-time first mate aboard the ship and one of the few crewmen to survive the haunting. Nelson was apparently fascinated as well as terrified by the ghost, and, by constantly making note of its appearances and disappearances, discovered something very unusual about the "thing." Every time a member of the crew died, the evil presence temporarily vanished from the ship. Sometimes it would be absent for a few days, while on other occasions it would be back within a few hours. Nonetheless, it always disappeared right after a death. Nelson began to realize that the crew were not necessarily killing themselves merely to escape the presence, but that the "thing" somehow *survived* by driving the men crazy with fear until they finally destroyed themselves.

And that's just about all we know about the *Ivan Vassilli* horror.

If you're a *Star Trek* fan, you will probably notice how similar this case is to the plot of one of their most ingenious episodes. If you recall, in one show the *Enterprise,* just like the *Ivan Vassilli,* was taken over by an invisible presence which was endowed with powerful psychic abilities. It, too, survived and literally "fed" on fear and hatred. Luckily, Captain Kirk was able to solve the mystery of the creature, just as Nelson apparently did, and exorcised it from his ship through the crew's laughter. Perhaps this *Star Trek* episode was more fact than fiction. In fact, I've often wondered just how the show's writers came up with their story line.

After her trip to San Francisco, the *Ivan Vassilli* returned to her home port in Russia and never sailed again. No sailor in his right mind would venture aboard her, much less sail with her on the open seas. The ship's sea-going days were obviously over, so it was eventually burned and the nightmare came to an end.

The strange story of the *Ivan Vassilli,* though, is not the only case of an evil haunting I have come across over the years. I wish it were, just as I wish I could assure you that all phantoms are about as dangerous as *Casper the Friendly Ghost.* But that wouldn't be an honest thing to say. All through the ages, a few unfortunate people have encountered evil presences in haunted houses, cemeteries, on mountain sides, and even in more unlikely places than that. This evil seems to be similar to that which stalked the *Ivan Vassilli.* For example, I encountered such an evil, for only a few seconds, in my own haunted house, and the experience was absolutely terrifying. So I know from first-hand experience just how real this "presence of evil" can be. Could evil be, then, a real physical force in the world? Does it have a psychic power of its own? Such cases as the accursed *Ivan Vassilli* make me think so; but, believe me, it isn't a very comforting feeling to know that evil forces are stalking the world ... perhaps continually seeking out human victims just as the *Vassilli* "thing" seemed to do. I would prefer *not* to believe it. Yet, many people have personally confronted just this same type of evil, and their stories make even the most spine-chilling fiction look pale by comparison. We cannot shut our eyes to the facts.

In 1977, for instance, I received a call from a Mr. Steve Gordon. (This isn't his real name, which he asked me to keep private.) He was a young man who was recovering from a motorcycle accident when he first called. But as I talked to him it became clear that something more horrible than the accident was preying on his mind.

He explained that, since he had to stay in bed for several weeks, he was staying with his mother in her rather modern tract home in a local southern California town rather close to my own home. His mother's house had never been haunted, he went on to say, but shortly after he moved in he started waking up at night and sensing a powerful and evil presence in the house. This presence would remain for only a few seconds, and then, as though someone had turned off a switch, it would simply vanish. Steve also told me that these "visitations" would occur maybe three or four times a night. And each time they did there was no mistaking the feeling of evil that overcame him. The evil seemed to saturate his entire room. However, the thing was afraid of light, he added, and if he left a light burning in the house at night he could get a good night's sleep. He had become so frightened by his experiences that he had contacted a local psychical research club and they had suggested that he call me.

At first I wasn't too impressed by Steve's story. After all, he had just undergone a serious accident, and I felt that perhaps the memories or terror of his ordeal were playing tricks on his mind. But then he told me something which I couldn't dismiss so easily. His mother, he said, could also feel the presence in the house. She, too, had begun waking up in the middle of the night with the feeling that some evil but totally invisible ghost was present with her. Often, Steve told me, they could both feel the presence at the same time. They never saw anything, though, but he felt sure that the force was related directly to the house. This had led him to check out the past history of the building as well as the land upon which it was built, and, so he claimed, he had found evidence that the entire tract was built on an old Indian burial ground. However, he never told me just where he picked up this bit of information, so the story struck me as more likely to be some local legend or gossip than fact.

Nonetheless, I could understand Steve's concern and worry. I couldn't help but think about the evil presence I had once felt in my own haunted home, so I knew that such things were possible and very, very frightening. What would it be like to live with such a thing and share your home with it? I still shudder when I even think about the possibility, so Steve had my full sympathy. But what could I do to help?

I told Steve that I knew of other such hauntings on record. I really didn't know quite what else to say. After all, I don't do exorcisms! (For some reason, people who contact psychic investigators tend to think that we either have the magical ability to exorcise spooks or have a ready-made way to de-haunt houses. I wish that were so!) However, I did suggest to him that, if he felt it would give him peace of mind, he might have his minister bless the house. It certainly couldn't do any harm, I explained. I also suggested that he call me if there were any further visitations, and I assured him that I would come out to the house myself if necessary and spend the night. I never heard from Steve again, so I guess everything worked out all right.

Even today, a year later, I still don't know what to make of Steve's story. His experience could have been real, totally imaginary, or perhaps he was just giving me the royal put-on. There's simply no way of telling. It would be easy to merely explain away Steve's experiences as due to some wild hallucination caused by his recent accident. But can we honestly do so? I don't think we can, since my young friend is only one of many people who have had this type of experience in a haunted house—as the following case further illustrates.

Reverend Le Leau and his wife, Esther, were a young couple with two small children and another baby on the way, when they came face to face with a most unpleasant haunted house in 1930. The ordeal began when they moved into a big, Southern-style house in Oklahoma. They had been house-hunting for weeks and this was just the sort of home they were looking for, with plenty of room inside, a big back porch, and a tree-shaded yard. It was a perfect home for the young family and they could hardly wait to move in. Little did they know that within a few months they would be fleeing from the house to save their very sanity. Even on the day they moved in, the Le Leaus were given a warning about the house when one of their children refused to play in one of the bedrooms. There was a ghost in it, he claimed, and he wasn't about to go near the place. But, of course, his parents didn't take him seriously.

As the days rolled by, though, Esther began to feel some awful presence in the house herself. It seemed to come from the central stairwell and would often move about. Although she couldn't see it, she could certainly feel it. The creature practically drove her crazy. It usually made its presence known in the house at night, during times when Reverend Le Leau was out taking care of church business. And, as the evening hours rolled by, the presence would begin to get stronger and stronger.

"As the evening progressed," writes Mrs. Le Leau in her diary on the case, "it grew stronger, until finally, I could time its actual arrival—10 p.m. exactly, it would be in the house waiting. And as the intensity grew and its animosity grew, the more clearly I could 'see' it—a tall, dark, faceless, shrouded presence, utterly evil, utterly vile. Just waiting and waiting and hating, there in the hall. And I would either sit in the study, or lie wide-awake in bed waiting and waiting and *willing* that *I'd not give way to fear,* for I knew if ever I did, all was lost."

Eventually, the haunting became such a strain on Mrs. Le Leau that she turned sickly. She became pale and lifeless, as though all her energy were being sucked out of her body.

Mrs. Le Leau was too frightened by the "thing" even to discuss her experiences with her husband. She tried to keep the ghost her own private secret. But gradually she came to realize that Reverend Le Leau could feel the presence too. In fact, by comparing notes, they later discovered that they both had been having very similar experiences. The ghost was no hallucination. Mrs. Le Leau wasn't going mad. It physically existed right in the house, and was every bit as real as the couple themselves. The presence even took on a sort of personal reality to Mrs. Le Leau.

"You would feel it creeping," she writes. "Later I could 'see' it standing in the hall. Vile. Evil. Sometimes, I thought that there was a terrible stench. My husband agrees to this, too. But so long as there was a light, and I did not yield to fear, it was helpless. But promptly, and my husband verifies this too, at 2 a.m. with the suddenness of a click of a light switch, it was gone and we could go to sleep. The danger was over until the next night."

Mrs. Le Leau couldn't figure out any way to fight the "thing." She prayed, placed Bibles all through the house, but nothing seemed to work. In fact, things got worse. Esther's health became seriously damaged and the Reverend couldn't even sleep a single night without being disturbed by nightmares. And every night, the presence would come back—stronger and stronger; just as hateful as ever.

The Le Leaus were left with no choice and decided to move out, but their last night was perhaps the worst of all. Again, to quote Mrs. Le Leau's testimony:

> We found a house in a matter of a few days, and were all packed, ready to move the next day except for my husband's books in the study. He was packing them the last night. I had grown so afraid in the house, I was even afraid for him to be up there alone doing that, and kept an ever apprehensive ear open for his cheery whistling. It grew later and later, and my apprehensions grew. His whistling had ceased, but I could hear him moving about. But the silence settled down and the whole house seemed to wait, and horror and terror and danger swept through the house all at once like a tide. There was a crashing rush of feet on the stairs, the door was literally hurled open, and my husband, white and panting, flung into the room. "My God," he gasped, "that damned thing came into the study just now."

I have little doubt that the Le Leaus really did encounter some horrible being in their Oklahoma house. I don't think they imagined it all. Although these events took place in 1930, Mrs. Le Leau didn't publish a full account of the haunting until 1951. Twenty years is a long time, so these experiences must have been extremely vivid to remain so firmly in her memory.

The couple's reactions to the ghost also strike me as being very similar to the ways in which the crew of the *Ivan Vassilli* responded to their horror. In both instances, the presence threw its victims into a state of sheer panic . . . a panic so overwhelming in the first instance that several of the crew killed themselves. Mrs. Le

Leau often seemed on the brink of this same state. She instinctively sensed that she must never become a slave to her own fear. For, as she wrote in her own words, " . . . I knew, if ever I did, all was lost." Apparently, in her own courageous way, she had figured out how to keep the ghoul at bay. It's too bad the *Ivan Vassilli* crew hadn't learned this same lesson. Evidently, this evil force seems to survive on *fear*. However, there are also other curious parallels between these cases. When I first read the Le Leaus' report, I was struck by the fact that they realized the ghost was powerless in the light. Steve made the same claim when he told me about the evil presence in his home. And the *Ivan Vassilli* "thing" also preferred lurking about at night in the darkness. Finally, the Le Leaus, Steve Gordon, and the crew of the *Ivan Vassilli* all felt that the evil presence never gradually left them. Instead, it always vanished in an instant, just like a light bulb blowing out.

Can all this be coincidence? Or did all these people confront a similar type of evil presence, although in different lands and at different times?

I know of at least two other ghost-hunters who have also encountered this type of momentary horror while investigating a haunted house. So even people trained to confront the psychic world are not immune from this type of force. Perhaps these types of "evil hauntings" are a lot more common than we might think!

Susy Smith is one of this country's leading writers on psychic phenomena. In fact, she has written three books on haunting alone, including *Ghosts Around the House* and *Haunted Houses for the Millions*. Susy, who has been a longtime friend of mine, is more than just a writer, though. She's also an investigator and has spent more than a few nights holding watch in haunted houses from coast to coast. Being a bit psychic herself makes Susy an ideal ghost-hunter.

In 1966, Susy made a grand tour of the United States in search of ghosts and haunted houses. And, according to what she writes in her *Ghosts Around the House,* she may have caught one or two! While on tour, she was particularly interested in investigating a house in Machias, Maine where a ghost has been appearing since 1799. However, Susy and her traveling companion actually encountered the ghost—or at least its presence—in their own motel room. It was a strange night, to say the least! Here's her story:

"We arrived in Machias around 8:30," writes Miss Smith, "and found a large room in the new, modern Bluebird Motel. . . Then we went out to dinner and returned at 10:00 o'clock. The moment I entered the motel room I began to feel light headed . . . I hurriedly prepared for bed, quite uncomfortably tired and dizzy."

However, sleep wasn't easy for Susy that night. Soon, some ungodly entity began to make itself known in the room, and she could psychically feel its presence:

"My head spun and I was approaching a condition of semi-consciousness as if I were being pulled forcibly into a whirlpool, when suddenly I became cold as if exposed to an icy blast . . . and my stomach began to tremble in fright."

Susy's traveling companion, Leah, could feel the presence too. To her, it felt as though something dreadful was in the room with them. Susy heartily agreed. Both of them could feel the bitter chilling feelings the ghost had brought into the room and with which it was attacking them. As Susy explains:

> We both felt some kind of negative presence in the room so strongly that we were badly frightened. We attempted to protect ourselves from its influence by repeating all the aphorisms for routing "evil spirits" that we could recall, and by praying and invoking the forces of good. Also, always a practical human being, I turned on the television and began to watch the "Johnny Carson Show," sure that laughter would bring me back to normal quicker than anything else.

The next day, Susy and Leah departed in further search of ghosts . . . but they never tried to investigate the one they had personally encountered the night before. Perhaps they were too scared. Nonetheless, Susy learned about a similar "evil haunting" the following year when she was called in to investigate a ghost holding forth in Miami, Florida. However, this haunted house was a little more conventional.

Like so many haunted houses, this one had a somewhat tragic history. A murder had taken place there five years before, on February 25, 1962, as a result of a family feud. The argument had been between Carrington H. Witherspoon, who owned the house and lived there with his family, and his teenage son. Just what the argument was about is a bit of a mystery, but it seems that young Witherspoon had gotten a young lady of his acquaintance "in trouble." Anyway, the elder Witherspoon tried to break a chair over his son's head at the height of the argument. He was a violent man to begin with, and often beat his wife and children. So there was nothing really unusual about the fight. But this one was the last straw as far as Mrs. Witherspoon was concerned. She pulled a gun and shot her husband right through the heart.

In 1965 the house fell into the hands of a new owner, a Mrs. Gladys Chapman, who moved in with a friend right after buying the place. Later, Mrs. C. Harvey White (Mrs. Chapman's daughter) and her family moved in and joined them as well. Everyone knew about the house's dreadful history, but no one was put off by it. Instead, the house's rather gruesome past and reputation was a frequent topic of conversation. It gave the old place a little "class," or so the occupants thought. But, I don't think they expected that a full-fledged ghost came along with it.

The ghost first started acting up shortly after the Whites moved in. To their annoyance, loud crashing or thumping noises would break out night after night between two and three in the morning. Later during their stay, they could hear what sounded like furniture being moved and scraped along the floor in the living room late at night. Much of the noise also seemed to come from another room in the house, a den area called the "Florida Room." Despite its name, though, this room was hardly sunny. In fact, it was downright gloomy and looked just like a perfect place for a ghost to live.

All these mysterious events were certainly annoying, but the families weren't too concerned about them. However, after living there awhile longer, Mrs. White began to sense the physical presence of the ghost.

"I could sometimes feel something right beside me although there was nothing to see," she told Miss Smith. "And particularly in the Florida Room I had chills and a feeling of evil. Occasionally at night I felt that someone was standing there, staring at me."

Mrs. White was sure that Witherspoon's ghost had returned to harass them. She also realized they needed help . . . and fast.

Susy visited the house personally and for the first time on May 31, 1967, and she brought along a psychic friend of hers to help with the investigation. The psychic soon became the evening's star performer. He, too, could sense "bad vibrations" in the Florida Room and tried to psychically pick up information about the ghost. He was somewhat successful at his job. He tuned in on the murder, described the foul deed and the murdered man in some detail, and even sensed Witherspoon's presence right in the house. Since everyone agreed that the old man's ghost was probably causing the haunting to begin with, the psychic tried to exorcise it. He shouted at the ghost, implored it to leave, threatened it, and so on, even though he couldn't actually see it. It was all a good show, but it really didn't seem to do much good and everyone felt that the exorcism had been a failure. So, Susy spent the rest of the evening just talking with the family, jotting down their experiences, and trying to calm them as best she could. But it looked like the ghost was there to stay.

That night, though, according to Susy's account, Mrs. White suddenly awoke around midnight. Once again she could feel the ghost's presence in the room with her, and, for the first time, she seemed to mentally tune in on the spook. By some type of telepathy between them, she began to understand the ghost instead of fearing it. She felt it was saying to her, "Please let me stay here. I have no place to go. I built this house. I don't want to leave."

The ghost never appeared in the house afterwards. The eerie and nightly noises stopped and no one ever felt an evil presence in the house again.

So this is one ghost story that is blessed with a happy ending. Not all ghosts, though, are so considerate.

Mrs. Le Leau and several of the crewmen aboard the *Ivan Vassilli* felt that their ghosts were somehow sucking the very life out of them. Even Reverend Le Leau could only look on helplessly as his wife's health simply gave out from under her. It became worse and worse the longer she stayed in the house. And Rose Despard, whose ghost was anything but nasty, knew that the "weeping woman" she saw often drew either energy or some sort of force from her in order to appear. Every so often you'll run across cases like these . . . hauntings in which the ghosts literally vampirize the living. These are perhaps the most vile and dangerous hauntings of all . . . hauntings that slowly drain the life from any victim trapped within their walls, like a spider weaving its web around a fly caught in its lair. Luckily, these cases are very rare, but they do exist, nonetheless. They represent the dark side of the occult world.

One of the most detailed accounts ever written about one such cruel haunting was reported to the American Society for Psychical Research many years ago and was published by them in 1920. The account was written by Mrs. Elizabeth Gladden Wood, who had lived in an accursed house with her husband for four long and troubled years.

On May 1, 1894, Mr. and Mrs. Benjamin Wood leased a twenty-five-year-old, three-story stone house in Brooklyn, New York. They were practical people. Both of them were in their fifties; they didn't consider themselves churchgoers by any means, and had little interest in the occult or the supernatural. They were just a pair of ordinary, everyday people like you and me, out to find a nice comfortable home for themselves. They eventually found a big house on W—— Street which fit the bill, so Mrs. Wood leased it with the hope that it might become a permanent home for them. In fact, she had leased it before her husband even had time to peek inside. (So you see, there were liberated women even back in those days!) She just knew that it was the right house for them.

Mr. Wood wasn't as enthusiastic about the house, though. As soon as he stepped inside the front door that fateful May day he sensed that there was something wrong in the place, and that the house just seemed to "dislike" him. As Mrs. Wood later recalled:

> Mr. Wood had never seen the interior until we moved in. He preceded me by about two hours. When I arrived, he told me that the house impressed him strangely and unpleasantly . . . he explained his remark by saying that as soon as he entered it, something told him it was a bad move and that he would die in the house. . .

Mrs. Wood couldn't understand her husband's reaction to the house. To her, it was just a nice old stone house. But gradually, she too began to sense some evil presence there. The following is from her report to the A.S.P.R.:

By the end of the first month we were fully agreed that there was a malignant force in the house. It was an intelligent force and pursued Mr. Wood with a devilish malice, through the four years of our stay until the fourth year was half gone. It was not a dominating force, compelling one to do a thing against his will, it was a force opposing and vindictive . . . In the house or out of it, the influence followed him. Accident after accident, bad luck in business, and a depression constant and overpowering, foiled every attempt he made to put aside the influence.

At first, the force attacked Mr. Wood in little ways. It pushed him over, slapped him about but—unlike the horror which stalked the Le Leaus' house—seemed to enjoy pulling its pranks in broad daylight. For instance, on one occasion Mr. Woods was lying peacefully on his living room couch when—zap!—some mysterious force literally threw him off onto the floor. On other occasions, the ghost took quite a delight in throwing the aging man to the floor or knocking him down as he bent over to tie his shoelaces. Mrs. Wood even once saw a chair shift position by itself just as her husband was about to sit in it. The chair pulled itself right from under him. The ghost even knocked her husband into a coal bin. He had gone to the cellar to get some coal when, as he later told his wife, he felt a human hand shove him right into the sooty mess as soon as he had bent over to reach into the bin.

However, the ghost also tried to communicate with the Woods and on several occasions called out Mrs. Wood's name clearly as though trying to catch her attention:

It wasn't exactly like a human voice yet the enunciation was very clear and distinct—perfect, in fact. It was a very peculiar voice, unlike any other that I ever heard. It had a metallic quality and it was impossible to say whether it was the voice of a man or a woman. It always seemed to come from out of doors, high up in the air, and directly overhead . . . The voice always called my name, nothing more and always twice, never more or less.

One evening in summer . . . we were sitting in the kitchen, which was a large and pleasant room. It was six o'clock. Both dogs were with me as usual. In the midst of our conversation, the voice called my name loud and clear as usual . . . "Mrs. Wood! Mrs. Wood!" I paid no attention but continued our conversation. Mr. Wood looked at me in surprise and told me that somebody was calling me, and asked me if I had not heard. I said with indifference, "That's the ghost." He insisted it was not possible, that it was surely a person. Just then it rang out again, louder and clearer than before: "Mrs. Wood! Mrs. Wood!" Both dogs barked at the second call, not as though frightened, but as though to tell us somebody was at the door. I then asked Mr. Wood whether the voice that called me was that of a man or woman. He thought for a moment and then said with a laugh as he looked up at me that he didn't know. It was his surrender. . .

The ghost also took on visible form, although these appearances were rare. Nonetheless, on several occasions Mr. Wood claimed that he had seen dark shadowy figures darting through the house.

Now so far, you might be saying to yourself, this case doesn't sound very evil at all. The ghost really didn't hurt anyone. Instead, it just seemed to be having a bit of fun by pulling some rather slapstick practical jokes. After all, who can resist giving a man bending over a coal bin a little shove? Or giving someone a kick in the pants just as he's about to fall asleep? On the other hand, perhaps the ghost was merely trying to make contact with the Woods. Pushing them about or calling Mrs.

Wood's name may have been the only way it could draw attention to itself.

However, as time went by the ghost became more sinister. To Mrs. Wood's horror, their ghostly practical joker became foul and evil, and started to wage an all-out war on her husband. There were times when it came close to killing the man. The ghost tried to make a window break loose from its frame and fall on his head; it broke a window pane so that the shattered and deadly glass almost fell right on top of him as he walked in the yard below; and on one occasion it threw Mr. Wood to the floor so forcefully that he was knocked cold. Then the ghost started to attack Mr. Wood more directly . . . it slowly tried to drain the very life out of him.

This ordeal began when Mr. Wood decided to move into the back parlor of the house. This was the one room of the house where the evil presence of the ghost could be felt most strongly. Even Mrs. Wood could sense the evil there.

"The room had always affected me unpleasantly," recalled Mrs. Wood in her report to the A.S.P.R. "It was the only room in the house that ever did. . . It was a delightful room under the gaslight, but in the daytime, although it was a bright and sunny room . . . I could not endure to enter it. A heavy, black, pall seemed to overhang the entire room suspended from about midway from the ceiling."

Although he knew that this was the ghost's very own room, Mr. Wood knew he had to fight the ghost everywhere he could. He wanted to defy the ghost, so he moved right into the room and refused to leave it for weeks. Gradually, though, he began to fall ill. It seems the ghost was having its revenge. He lost his appetite, couldn't eat or drink a thing, and began to lose weight until he was little more than a skeleton. Each day he grew weaker and weaker. Even the doctor was totally baffled by the illness. He couldn't find any medical cause for the sickness and finally gave up on the case altogether, explaining to the Woods that there was nothing more he could do. However, Mr. Wood stuck it out. He refused to budge from the room and verbally defied the ghost, swearing he would never buckle under its power. Then, slowly but surely, his health improved.

As Mrs. Wood specifically notes in her report, after her husband regained his health the ghost never again tried to attack him. It merely went back to pulling the little annoyances and practical jokes that it had perpetrated when they first moved in. By this time, though, the Woods had been intrigued enough by the haunting to trace the history of the house, hoping to discover just who was haunting them and why it was so vicious. It was during this hunt that the Woods uncovered some peculiar information about the house.

First, they discovered that the back parlor, which had almost killed Mr. Wood, was the very room in which the previous tenant had died. But was he the ghost? Or was he the ghost's previous victim? The Woods never found out for sure. But they did find out something else very strange about the parlor. *Other* tenants, in fact several of them, had also died there!

In May, 1898, the Woods finally moved from the house when their lease expired. They refused to renew it and as soon as they left the place Mr. Wood's health improved even further and his business took several turns for the better. Finally after four years, it appeared that the Woods were free. The house would have to find itself a different victim.

5. POLTERGEISTS, OR "NOISY GHOSTS"

Poltergeist (pronounced pōl'-tr-gīst) is a very odd-sounding German word that is often used by ghost-hunters. Roughly translated, it means something like "noisy ghost" or "rackety spirit". The term *poltergeist,* though, is only used by psychical investigators to describe one very special type of haunting. As you will see, these cases are quite different from your more conventional or ordinary haunted houses in many ways. They can also be much more exciting.

So just what is a poltergeist? Instead of trying to give you a definition, it might be easier to simply describe a typical case.

One of the most famous poltergeist hauntings ever recorded broke out in February, 1939 in England, and plagued the home of Mr. and Mrs. L. Forbes and their teenage son. Their two-story house was located right outside of London in a pretty suburb called Thornton Heath. (If you ever go to London, you'll drive right past Thornton Heath as you make your way from Gatwick Airport to downtown London.) The house had no reputation for being haunted; but nonetheless on the evening of February 19 it suddenly became the scene of almost vicious ghostly activity which rampaged for weeks and nearly wrecked the place. Household furniture flew about, glasses threw themselves out of cabinets or jumped and exploded in midair, and knickknacks floated through the air as though carried by some unseen hand.

Many poltergeists like to begin their attacks at night,

and this one was no different. Both Mr. and Mrs. Forbes had gone to bed that fateful February evening and had just turned off the light when they heard a sudden crash next to their bed. It sounded as if glass had been shattered in the room. They turned the light on to see what had caused the curious sound and discovered that a glass which Mrs. Forbes usually kept on a little bedside table had somehow fallen to the floor. This rather unnerved Mrs. Forbes, since she was certain that she hadn't knocked the table in the dark.

But even as the Forbes sat there puzzled, trying to figure out how the glass could have fallen, the next bit of poltergeistery broke out. Another glass suddenly came sailing through the air and almost bashed into them. The couple just sat there for a moment after this incident, almost stunned.

Mr. Forbes was understandably concerned about the flying glassware, but suggested that they turn off the lights once again and see what would happen in the dark. They didn't have long to wait. No sooner had they clicked off the lights then their quilt started to jump up and down on their bed. Mr. Forbes tried to turn the light back on to find out what was making the quilt act so strangely, but discovered to his amazement that the bulb was missing! Somehow it had unscrewed itself, and it was later found placed in a chair near their bed.

These tricks went on for quite awhile, but things settled down again by midnight or so and this rest gave the Forbes a chance to get a decent night's sleep. The very next morning, though, new and even more disturbing phenomena broke out. Eggs from the refrigerator flew about; glasses jumped off counters or out of shelves and crashed to the floor; and some of them exploded into millions of pieces as if tiny bombs were inside of them.

Finally, the Forbes had had enough, and in desperation they called the local newspapers and just about everyone else they thought might be able to explain the odd manifestations which were occurring in their home. In the meantime, the poltergeist kept up its rackety nuisance all day long.

That the Forbeses called in news reporters shouldn't strike you as strange. I've learned over the years that many people, when faced with a poltergeist in their home, will usually call any one of three places. Either they call the local police, thinking that some prankster or prowler has broken into their house and is causing the disturbance; or they call a minister or priest in the hope that he might be able to exorcize the house of "evil spirits"; or they call their local newspaper. I don't really know why poltergeist victims like to call in the press so much. I guess they feel that newspaper reporters have probably come up against just about everything imaginable during the course of their work, and are more likely than anyone else to figure out some likely explanation for this type of disturbance.

As soon as the press got wind of the case, though, all London learned about the poltergeist. Newspaper after newspaper carried stories about the haunted house and what their reporters had seen there. However, the newsmen were just as puzzled by the mysterious phenomena plaguing the Thornton Heath house as were the Forbeses themselves. So these investigators didn't really resolve anything.

The case really came to the public's attention a few days later when the London *Sunday Pictorial*, which had sent two reporters to the scene of the action, ran the following headlines: "GHOSTS WRECK HOME, FAMILY TERRORISED." Part of their story read as follows:

Two *Sunday Pictorial* representatives yesterday spent the most amazing day of their lives in a house in Thornton Heath, where some malevolent ghostly force is working miracles. They saw saucers—held in a woman's hand—smashed to smithereens by an invisible force. Eggs, saucepans, fenders, rugs, wineglasses, coal and a score of other objects sailed through the air before them—and sometimes through doors!—propelled by no human force.

This story must have taken the Londoners of 1939 quite by surprise. These were not idle ghost stories, Halloween-type pranks, or some sort of April Fool's joke. According to the *Pictorial* story, two of their most skeptical reporters, Victor Thompson and Lionel Crane, had seen these psychic wonders for themselves. One of them reported to the *Pictorial's* readers that he had seen an egg fly out of the kitchen and sail right into the living room where he was standing. Later that day, according to the lengthy news account, both writers heard a loud crash in the hallway of the house when everyone, including the Forbeses, were in the living room. On investigating the strange noise, they discovered that a fireplace screen had somehow thrown itself down the stairs from a second-story bedroom.

One of the reporters admitted in print that he had watched even more remarkable things. "While we were still standing in the hall a sharp-edged can opener lifted up from a table in the kitchen and sailed past Crane's head," Thompson reported.

The paper's editors was so intrigued by the newsmen's report that they immediately sent out another news team, consisting of no less than five writers, to see what they could dig up. An even more sensational story was run the very next day.

As one of the writers, who was made a Special Correspondent on the case, reported back to his office:

I was skeptical when I arrived at the house about 11 p.m. on Saturday. At seven o'clock on Sunday morning I was bewildered.

An egg-cup had shattered in my hand as I held it. A glass 'leapt' from a table. A foot-square mirror hurtled from the wall. Another egg-cup shattered on the ceiling, and Mrs. Forbes 'hurtled' across the room. All five of us saw these things. It was uncanny, but each of us formed our own conclusions. Three of us cannot make up our minds whether or not a human agency is responsible. The other two are definite that there is nothing 'spooky' in this villa. It was dawn when we left the house, bewildered, but all satisfied on one point . . . that whatever the force is, it is centered round frail, invalid Mrs. Forbes.

Most parapsychologists, including myself, follow the newspapers very carefully. You will be surprised how many poltergeist cases receive little back-page stories now and then in such papers as the *Los Angles Times,* the *Chicago Tribune* and other major city dailies. Following the papers is one good way of discovering, and tracking down, promising cases.

Sure enough, news reports about the Thornton Heath haunting soon came to the attention of Dr. Nandor Fodor, one of London's leading psychic investigators. Fodor was also the director of research of the London-based International Institute for Psychical Research, and he wasted no time before setting off to investigate the case on behalf of the Institute. The first thing he did, though, was to send out his research assistant, L.A. Evans, to look into the matter and decide whether further investigation was needed. Evans was only an amateur and part-time investigator but, nonetheless, a very competent and thorough one, and he became the first trained investigator to witness what was going on in the house.

Evans arrived at the Forbeses' house on February 23, while the poltergeist was still in full swing. As he reported back to Fodor:

I took the first opportunity of looking over the house. Mrs. Forbes came with me and pointed out the various objects and pieces of furniture which had been displaced and damaged. It is worth noting at this time that according to her story all the violence that had taken place appeared to have been directed at her. Time and again I was shown various chairs, rugs, a fire screen, etc, which she stated "had been thrown at her". Also a most definite point was made of the fact that at that time objects in the process of being "thrown" did not travel quickly but on the contrary appeared to float. Later on they moved at tremendous speed and, in the case of the wineglasses, too quickly to be followed.

Evans didn't have to wait long before the poltergeist acted up right in his own presence. In fact, according to his notes, the poltergeist gave the investigator a rather warm welcome:

I was shown the back bedroom. . . I particularly noticed over the mantelpiece on a shelf a white china cat which was broken and was standing between two blue pottery vases about six inches high. There were only the three pieces on the shelf. I commented on the broken cat and Mrs. Forbes told me that it had been thrown down the stairs the night before . . . We left the room together and came downstairs at once. Mrs. Forbes went into the kitchen and I joined the reporters in the front room standing with my back to the door, which was fully open. In about one minute there was a crash against the side of the grandfather clock (which stood at the foot of the stairs) and I at once went to see what it was. I had to walk only about three yards and I was there before Mrs. Forbes came out of the kitchen. It was a blue vase broken into seventeen pieces. I ran upstairs ahead of anyone and back into the bedroom and found only one of the two blue vases. . . .

While I was upstairs two loud crashes were heard

from the front room we had just left. The only inhabitants who were downstairs at the time were two friends of the Forbes, who were in the back room. They were in the act of coming out into the hall as I ran down the stairs. In the front room a large glass salad bowl was in pieces in the fireplace and a wineglass lay broken in the sideboard.

That night, Evans stayed in the house with the Forbeses to see if anything else would happen. He wasn't disappointed and was able to witness one most extraordinary phenomenon.

At the time, he and Mr. and Mrs. Forbes were sitting in the living room having a drink or two around a cozy fire. Mrs. Forbes was seated only three feet away from the investigator and was casually drinking from her glass. Suddenly, as she was about to take another sip, the glass tore itself from the startled woman's hand with a loud "pinging" sound and broke in half while in mid-air right over Evans's head. His report continues:

I at once asked her to try again, and handed her an exactly similar glass to the first, except this time it was empty. She sat in the same position holding it in the same manner as before. I watched it intently and exactly ten minutes later there was another "ping" quite as loud as the first and this was followed by the glass breaking on the floor at our feet. Although I know I never took my eyes off her hand and the glass, I also know I did not see it go. The first indication I had was the noise as in the first place. It would seem as though it went so quickly it deceived the eye. The glass was literally smashed to tiny pieces, and this in itself was abnormal, as it landed on a rug, and the distance from her hand to the floor was not more than two feet. . . .

After receiving Evans's report, Fodor decided to investigate the case personally. In fact, his investigation was so thorough that he was able to write a 222-page book entitled *On the Trail of the Poltergeist* just about this case alone. You'll have to read this book for yourself to learn about the Forbeses' poltergeist and how Fodor tracked it down and discovered the very cause of these mysterious PK attacks. It's a great mystery story, so I won't ruin it for you by telling you the ending. However, one incident which occurred during Fodor's investigation was so thrilling that I can't help but quote it.

Fodor first arrived at the Forbeses' house on February 24th. During the first day of his visit he was able to watch a chair fly at Mrs. Forbes from an empty room and to witness several cups flinging about by themselves. But the really fancy poltergeistery only occurred later that day when a friend of his, Dr. G.A.P. Wills, arrived to help in the investigation. Wills was standing with Mrs. Forbes in the kitchen helping her prepare tea when this almost unbelievable event took place:

> Mrs. Forbes was standing facing the sink filling the kettle from the tap. The kettle was in her left hand, her right was on the tap. Mr. Forbes, just returned from work, had taken off his collar and was in the act of placing it with his left hand on the table. I was standing talking to Mr. Forbes when absolutely without any ... movement on anyone's part ... a saucer appeared at two-thirds of the height of the door from the floor. . . It remained in this position for a split second, but long enough to identify it as a saucer. It then split in half with a loud crack, and fell vertically to the floor.

To make a long story short, these PK incidents erupted in the Forbeses' household for several weeks, day after day. They focused directly on Mrs. Forbes, as the newsmen had first noticed, and would even follow her if she left the house. If she went out shopping, for instance, the PK was very likely to break out in the store or market. Life certainly wasn't easy for the couple during these weeks, but the phenomena gradually occurred less and less frequently. Finally, they just stopped—as mysteriously as they had begun.

So, now you know what a poltergeist is. It's a very special kind of haunting which creates noisy and destructive disturbances in the house it is attacking. Most poltergeists take great delight in throwing and breaking things. However, poltergeist phenomena can be extremely varied. Like more conventional hauntings, no two cases are exactly alike. But the following types of PK disturbances are most often employed during poltergeist attacks:

1. *Object-throwings*. As just mentioned, the poltergeist loves to throw things; glasses, hardware, figurines, and just about anything else it can lay its hands on. In most cases, these household items will just jump up in the air and either float about or fly quickly as though thrown by a slingshot. For some reason, many poltergeists take particular pleasure in smashing objects, such as glass and china, against walls and furniture. Yet in other cases they will deliberately throw glasses or other fragile houseware against walls or onto the floor, but these items—for some totally bizarre reason—will *not* break. At other times the poltergeist will throw things right at the people living in the house or at visitors, often at full speed. However, these collisions rarely hurt anyone. Many people who have been struck by poltergeist-thrown objects report that, even though the objects were flying at top speed, they just seemed to "bounce off them" mysteriously and without hurting a bit. Even more amazing, sometimes an object hurled at a person by a poltergeist will suddenly stop in midair. It will then just float in front of the startled onlooker and will then fall harmlessly at his feet.

So, it looks as though the poltergeist likes to scare

people more than it wants to hurt anybody.

2. *Rappings*. When not throwing things, the poltergeist likes to pound on walls and make a considerable racket. This is probably the reason why these types of disturbances were called *poltergeists* ("noisy ghosts") in the first place. And noisy they can be! Sometimes these thumping or rapping sounds are like gentle tappings; yet they can become very loud and even sound like explosions. An investigator I know once heard a tremendous "rap" in a poltergeist house while sitting in the kitchen. He actually thought that a car had crashed through a living room wall. I know of another poltergeist that banged the walls of a house so violently that it put a six-foot-long crack in the ceiling.

3. *Stone-throwings*. Sometimes poltergeists will throw stones at the house it is attacking. In many cases, these stones will fall on the roof one after another, as though falling out of the sky, or will suddenly "materialize" *inside* the house and fly around breaking everything in sight.

4. *Fire-raising*. Just like little children, some poltergeists like to play with fire. There are many cases on file during which a poltergeist has started fire after fire in its victim's house. Sometimes dozens of fires will break out in just one day. In most cases, the poltergeist will not start them by using anything as earthly as matches. More often than not, "fire" poltergeists will make curtains, furniture, laundry and what not, just spontaneously burst out into flames. These objects don't even have to be burnable. In one case reported only a few years ago, wet laundry and a loaf of bread instantaneously broke out in flames!

The poltergeist can create other ghostly disturbances, as well. It can create disembodied voices, make water rain inside a house, and it can even cause objects to disappear into thin air and then make them reappear days later.

Oddly enough, some poltergeists will restrict themselves to just one form of attack; that is, some poltergeists will *just* throw things, others will *just* pound on walls or start fires, and so forth. Other more bizarre poltergeists, though, will create all sorts of sometimes violent phenomena. It is not rare, in this respect, for a poltergeist to do everything from throwing objects, to dematerializing household items, to starting fires in the course of its attack. Even other poltergeists will act very differently. They will start by employing only one type of PK attack, such as stone-throwing, and then sometime later will change over and start using a very different form of nuisance. In 1974, for example, a poltergeist raged in Michigan which began by banging on the walls. After awhile the poltergeist apparently got bored with that so it started throwing things. Finally it began starting fires all over the place and practically burned down the house.

As you can see, a poltergeist is very different from an ordinary haunted house in many respects. You may have spotted a few of these differences yourself as you read over the Thornton Heath case. There are, in fact, four major differences between the poltergeist and a haunted house. So let's take a look at each of these in turn.

To begin with, poltergeists create slightly different phenomena from what you would normally encounter in a more conventional haunted house. As I pointed out in Chapter 1, when investigating a haunting you will usually run into such things as apparitions (or "ghosts"), or hear strange noises such as phantom footsteps, smell strange odors, or feel invisible presences in the place. But poltergeists are much more dynamic. They don't play around with that kid stuff! They like to create really lively disturbances! Haunted houses usually don't make that much noise.

Secondly, and most important of all, poltergeists always focus on (or center around) a *person*. When a home and family are being bothered by a poltergeist, the

PK will usually *only occur when a certain member of the household is present*. If that person leaves the house, the PK will stop. Yet, it will start right back up again as soon as he or she comes home. The poltergeist may even follow this person if he or she leaves the house. If the entire family moves to a new house, the poltergeist will usually follow right along with them. So, unlike a haunting, you can't run away from a poltergeist.

Now, just who is it who is usually victimized by a poltergeist? In more cases than not, "poltergeist people" are youngsters or teenagers between the ages of eleven and seventeen. Of course, some adults become poltergeist victims too (like Mrs. Forbes) but these cases are much rarer. In fact, in about two-thirds of all recorded poltergeist hauntings, the PK focused on a youngster. So you might say that poltergeists are very special hauntings which are usually attracted to young people. Later, I'll explain just why this happens.

In summary, then, there's a very good rule of thumb to distinguish a poltergeist from a regular haunted house. Hauntings focus on a *place;* poltergeists focus on a *person.*

A third major difference between poltergeists and hauntings concerns the time span of the attack. If you recall, hauntings can go on for years. Some have been active for two or three hundred years, in fact. But just about all poltergeists are very short affairs. A typical case rarely lasts for more than a few weeks or months, and some are even shorter than that. And once the poltergeist stops its attack, it rarely returns.

Finally, poltergeists don't seem to have very much to do with ghosts at all. Apparitions are only very, very rarely seen during these attacks. The house in which the poltergeist occurs practically never has any history of tragedy, or any other "ghostly" reputation. So we might say that while hauntings seem to be caused by some sort of "being" or "ghost," poltergeists seem to be created by some invisible type of energy or force. They may break and throw things, but not very many of them show any real intelligence like some ghosts do.

With all these facts in mind, let's take a look at a couple of recent poltergeist reports.

One of the world's leading poltergeist experts is Professor Hans Bender. Dr. Bender is a German psychologist and for years has headed a special parapsychology division at the University of Freiburg. He has probably investigated and witnessed more poltergeist cases than any other parapsychologist in the business. Bender has also come up against some real stumpers. You see, not all poltergeists are as clear-cut as the Thornton Heath one. Some will begin their attacks not by throwing things or knocking on walls, but by making household appliances or electrical gadgets malfunction. Sometimes it takes a real expert to know when a poltergeist is active, at least at first. The following is a good case in point.

In 1967, Bender and his co-workers were called in to investigate a poltergeist outbreak in the small, quiet town of Rosenheim in Bavaria. This poltergeist wasn't attacking a home, but was running loose in a lawyer's office. At first, though, the poltergeist was very sneaky and secretly disrupted the office by making phones go haywire, blowing fuses, and causing other electrical problems. Time and time again the lights in the office would blink on and off, light bulbs exploded for absolutely no reason, and even phones would ring without cause.

At first, the lawyer and his office staff thought that the disturbances had a normal explanation. After all, they probably didn't know what a poltergeist was, so they weren't expecting one. So they did the most obvious thing; they called in experts from the local power company to check over the office's electrical system. The experts went over every conceivable fuse, wire, and power source, but could find nothing wrong. Finally, they even cut off the power to the building altogether and hooked it up to an emergency power unit. This, however, made little difference to the poltergeist, and electrical disturbances continued to plague the office. In fact, sometimes the power unit itself would be affected by some unknown energy. By now the experts were just as stumped as everyone else.

It was about this time that Dr. Bender became involved in the case, and made a personal investigation of the Rosenheim disturbances. It didn't take him long to isolate the cause of the phenomena. He discovered that they only took place when a teenage worker, Annemarie Schnabel, was present in the offices. Sometimes the disturbances would occur, as Bender himself witnessed, as soon as the girl walked into the office to begin work. According to the psychologist:

When this young girl walked through the gangways, [halls] the lamps behind her began to swing. . . If bulbs exploded, the fragments flew towards her. . .

The discovery of the PK nature of the occurrences led to an intensification of the events: paintings began to swing and to turn, drawers came out by themselves, documents were displaced, a . . . cabinet moved twice . . . from the wall, etc. etc. Annemarie Sch., [got] more and more nervous. . . When she was sent on leave, nothing happened, and when she definitely left the offices for a new position, no more disturbances occurred. But similar events, less obvious and kept secret, happened for some time in the new office where she was working.

So in this case, it seems that once Bender proved that a poltergeist was active, the PK became more ghostlike. In other words, the poltergeist came out of hiding.

I was able to discuss the Rosenheim case with Dr. Bender personally in 1969 when I met him at a parapsychology meeting in New York. During our meeting, he gave me some added information on the case. On one occasion, he said, a group of newsmen were visiting the Rosenheim offices along with some local sightseers. The newsmen were there to film a story on the poltergeist. While they were filming, some of the visitors thought they saw a vapory, ghostlike form, somewhat resembling a disembodied arm, appear suddenly out of a vent on the floor. It zoomed up, according to them, and crashed into a painting on a nearby wall. Upon impact, the picture began to swing back and forth. Luckily, some of the film crew also saw this bizarre event, and, since their cameras were all set to go, they were able to catch the painting as it swung.

The United States has its own resident poltergeist-chaser, too. As pointed out in Chapter 2, the Psychical Research Foundation in Durham, North Carolina actively investigates haunted houses. They also track down poltergeists. In fact, W.G. Roll, as director of the Foundation, specializes in these cases. In his book *The Poltergeist,* which was published just a few years ago, he tells about no less than six cases he has personally investigated. Due to space, though, only one will be summarized here.

In February, 1958 a poltergeist broke out in the home of Mr. and Mrs. James Herrmann of Seaford, New York. (The case, in fact, was the first one Roll ever investigated personally.) The Herrmanns had two children; Jimmy (who was twelve) and Lucille (aged thirteen). At first, bottles mysteriously popped their caps off, and then fell over by themselves. These "bottle poppings," as they were called, would even occur in empty rooms. Then bottles all over the house started throwing themselves off shelves. Next, small household items started sliding across shelves and sometimes fell to the floor as though pulled by invisible strings. A few small objects even began to fly through the house as though slung by a catapult. Needless to say, the Herrmanns were totally mystified by the phenomena.

At first the Herrmanns didn't know what to do about the disturbances, so on February 9th, only a few days after the manifestations had begun, they called in the local police, who made a thorough search of the house. They hoped to find some normal explanation for the odd things going on, but could find nothing unusual, although they were able to witness some of the PK for themselves. Ultimately, the police issued a report on their investigation in which they just about admitted that they couldn't solve the case. Quoted below is a part of this first official police report. (I like to use these reports because police investigators are usually very thorough and precise in their work. The term "complainant" refers to Mr. Herrmann.)

On Sunday, Feb. 9th, 1958, at about 1015 hours [10:15 a.m.] the whole family was in the dining room of the house. Noises were heard to come from different rooms and on checking it was found that the holy water bottle on the dresser in the master bedroom had again opened and spilled. A new bottle of toilet water on another dresser in the master room had fallen, lost its screw cap and also a rubber stopper and the contents were spilled. At the same time a bottle of shampoo and a bottle of Kaopectate in the bathroom had lost their caps, fallen over and were spilling their contents. The starch in the kitchen was also opened and spilled again and a can of paint thinner in the cellar had opened, fallen and was spilling on the floor. The complainant then called the police department and Patrolman J. Hughes of the 7th Precinct responded. While Patrolman Hughes was at the complainant's home, all the family was present with him in the living room when noises were heard in the bathroom. When Patrolman Hughes went into the bathroom with the complainant's family he found the medicine and the shampoo had again spilled. The complainant further stated that at the time of occur-

rences there were no tremors in the house, no loud
noises or disturbances of any kind that could be noticed. None of the appliances were going at these
times and the complainant has no high frequency
equipment at all in the house.

Even though no one could figure out what was causing the phenomena, neither the Herrmanns nor the police sensed at first that anything psychic was going on in
the house. They thought that perhaps someone was using a ham radio in the neighborhood which was setting
up some type of weird electrical disturbance. Unfortunately, this theory couldn't explain why the Herrmanns' neighbors weren't having any of the same problems. The disturbances were clearly centering just in the
Herrmann's home. The Herrmanns also thought that
maybe the house's own power system had gone haywire.
Some local officials even thought that perhaps an underground stream was flowing near the house and was causing it to rumble about. However, none of these explanations fit the facts.

Shortly after the disturbances began, however, both
Mr. and Mrs. Herrmann witnessed a series of startling
events which they *knew* could not possibly have a normal explanation. For instance, one morning Mr. Herrmann was standing near the bathroom watching his
twelve-year-old son, Jimmy, brushing his teeth, when
two bottles which were standing on a table began to
move. One slid across the small table slowly as though
pulled by a string, while the other spun around by itself.

Another witness to these strange events was Mrs.
Marie Murtha, a cousin of the Herrmanns who first
confronted the poltergeist when she visited the house on
February 15th, about a week and a half after the disturbances first began. At one time during her visit, she
was sitting in the living room with Jimmy when her attention was caught by a little statue on the coffee table.
Right before her eyes it began to "wiggle" about and

then shot into the air and flew about two feet before falling to the floor.

Sometimes these flights would occur one after another. For example, there was a rash of these incidents on February 20th. Again, to quote from the police report filed on the case:

On the above date [February 20th] at about 2145 hours [9:45 p.m.] Mrs. Herrmann was on the phone in the dining room, James was right next to her and Lucille was in the bedroom. James was putting his books away and there was a bottle of ink on the south side of the table. A very loud pop was heard and the ink bottle lost its screw top and the bottle left the table in a northeasterly direction. The bottle landed in the living room and the ink spilled on the chair, floor and on the wallpaper on the north side of the front door. Mrs. Herrmann immediately hung up and called the writer, who had left the house about 10 minutes prior to this occurrence. When the writer arrived it was learned that as soon as Mrs. Herrmann called, she had taken the two children with her into the hallway to await the arrival of the writer. At about 2150 hours [9:50 p.m.] while the children were with her a loud noise was again heard in the living room. All three of them went into the room and found the male figurine had again left the end table and had again flown through the air for about 10 feet and again hit the desk about six inches to the east of where it had hit the first time. On this occurrence the only noise heard was when the figurine hit the desk and at this time it broke into many pieces and fell to the floor. At this time the only appliance running was the oil burner and no one was again in the room.

W.G. Roll and another investigator arrived in Seaford on March 10th. This was over a month after the disturbances had begun. Since the PK was already beginning to die out by this time, the investigators were a little late to witness any of the fancier PK. But, they did interview every witness they could find and analyzed everything that had happened in the house. They wanted to make sure that some of the PK had occurred during times when both the Herrmann children could be accounted for.

Roll and his colleague, J. Gaither Pratt, discovered that during the previous month no less than twenty-three bottle poppings had occurred, and that the poltergeist had thrown household objects on at least forty occasions. Luckily, Roll was able to witness one PK event himself during his short stay at the house. The following is from his book *The Poltergeist:*

> Gaither and I were present in the house during one of the bottle poppings. In the evening of March 10, at 8:14 p.m. when I was sitting at the dining room table and Gaither was in the living room, there was a loud, dull noise which sounded as if it came from the floor or lower wall of the kitchen-bathroom area. Jimmy was in the bathroom, Lucille was in bed, and Mrs. Herrmann was in the master bedroom coming toward the central hallway (Herrmann was away). I investigated upstairs, and Gaither went down to the cellar. Here he found a bleach bottle in a cardboard box by the washing machine which had lost its cap and had fallen over against the side of the box. The cap was on the floor in back of the box. The bottle was only partially full, and the bleach had not spilled.
>
> The cap had fallen right side up, it was still wet inside and there was a wet spot on the floor below it.

After investigating this strange event, Roll and Pratt tried to figure out a way to make bottles "pop their tops" normally and experimented to see if any chemicals placed inside could make pressure build up and create a similar effect. They tested everything from dry ice to carbon dioxide. While they succeeded in blowing up a bottle or two, they were never able to duplicate what the poltergeist could do.

By this time, though, the poltergeist was over. The whole haunting only lasted a short five weeks. But Roll and Pratt did discover one very interesting thing about the Seaford disturbances. Whenever any PK broke out, young Jimmy Herrmann was always home! It therefore became clear to the investigators that Jimmy was somehow linked to the poltergeist. For some reason, it needed his presence in the house before it could cause the object-throwings and bottle-poppings. No disturbances ever occurred, they found out by rechecking their notes, when Jimmy was out of the house or asleep. Of course, these facts immediately suggested that perhaps Jimmy was faking the PK. However when confronted, he refused to admit that he had anything to do with the disturbances.

Roll and Pratt tended to agree. After all, they noted, many of the PK incidents had occurred when Jimmy was being carefully watched, or they occurred in totally empty rooms. Nor did they think that any electrical or seismic (earthquake) activity could explain the mysterious events which had so bothered the Herrmanns. In short, they believed that a poltergeist was most likely the cause of the Seaford disturbances.

So we can see that in all the cases summarized in this chapter the poltergeist always focused on one person in the distressed household. The Thornton Heath poltergeist literally attacked Mr. Forbes; the Rosenheim geist only broke out when Annemarie came to work; and the Seaford disturbances seemed directly linked to Jimmy. This same pattern crops up in case after case. For example, in 1961, W.E. Cox, a well-known expert on psychokinesis, analyzed some forty-six poltergeist reports and found that the disturbances were linked to a specific person in the afflicted homes in over two-thirds of the cases. And, in most of these cases, the "poltergeist agents" were children. (Cox's report was published in the April, 1961 issue of the *Journal* of the American Society for Psychical Research.)

Obviously, facts like these are telling us something very important about the nature of the poltergeist, and they prompt us to ask some very thought-provoking questions: Why does the presence of these children seem necessary before a poltergeist can erupt? Why do only *certain* children become poltergeist victims? And why does the poltergeist often follow these young people—and their families—if they try to run away from the disturbances?

These are the very questions parapsychologists are now asking themselves. And we may just have the answers to them. Most parapsychologists believe that, somehow, *these children or agents are actually producing the poltergeist attacks themselves!* Let me explain this a little more thoroughly.

As you probably know, a few very gifted people can make objects move just by concentrating on them. Maybe you have even seen films of psychics moving glasses or other small objects to and fro just by staring at them and willing them to move. This is, of course, the power of mind-over-matter. (Remember, the technical term for this power is *psychokinesis.*) Somehow, each of us probably has a bit of this mind-over-matter energy within our own minds and bodies even though we can't control it to any great extent. However, many people—who are not, or do not consider themselves to be, psychic—are able to do little psychic things with this ability. Many of us, for instance, can roll dice and make them land on a certain face more often than coincidence can account for. And a few people are so gifted with this ability that they can even levitate tables. Right now, news stories are coming out of the Soviet Union about a man who can lift a book or rubber ball into the air, remove his hands, and make the objects float there for several seconds just by the power of his mind.

Now, many parapsychologists also believe that some people might be able to use this "energy," or whatever psychokinesis is, *unconsciously*. That is, perhaps some of us can use our mind-over-matter abilities without even knowing it. Let me cite an example.

One day about a year ago I was writing about Uri Geller, a well-known psychic from Israel, who can make keys and other metal objects bend just by willing it to happen. Usually he will take a common everyday house key and either rub it a bit or merely stare at it. And sure enough, sometimes it will bend. Well, as I said, I had been writing about Uri Geller all day, so he and his powers were very much on my mind later on when I went to lunch with a friend. We started talking about Geller while waiting for our food to arrive, and just for fun I reached into my pocket, took out my keys, and started to toy with them. Suddenly, one of my own keys bent psychically! I wasn't "willing'" it to happen. I wasn't even sure that anybody except Uri Geller could even do such a thing. However without my even knowing it, I had used my own PK—which I didn't know I had to this extent—to bend the key. For a moment, I became psychic in spite of myself.

So you see, PK can occur when we least expect it. It doesn't only occur when we want it to. It can happen totally spontaneously.

Now just think. What would happen if all of a sudden you became very psychic, even though you didn't realize it, and your PK started acting up all over the place? Your PK might run around your house throwing things, pounding on walls, breaking furniture, etc. In other words, you would probably let loose a poltergeist! This is probably just what happens during a poltergeist case. Most likely, someone in the household is using his own PK powers without even knowing it and is causing all the uproar. That's why the poltergeist will follow the family if they try to run away from their home. Poltergeists, therefore, have very little to do with ghosts, spirits of the dead, or haunted houses. Instead, it seems that most poltergeists are actually caused by living people.

But why are only certain people, especially young adults, able to create poltergeists? And why are these attacks so destructive? Parapsychologists think they have the answers to these questions also.

We owe much of our understanding about the poltergeist to W.G. Roll and his co-workers. As pointed out earlier, Roll and his team have investigated several cases and have studied a number of young people who seem able to produce these outbreaks. After several years of research Roll discovered that these agents all share one thing in common: they all have very similar personalities. They were all unhappy, very hostile towards their parents or the people with whom they lived, and were very frustrated and aggressive inside. However, these children were also very reserved. In other words, they refused to express their feelings openly by throwing tantrums, or answering back, or picking on the family dog! They kept their true feelings bottled up inside themselves.

Just think back for a minute. When you were younger, no doubt you were scolded every so often by your parents. And no doubt you were very angry when this happened. But what could you do about it? You couldn't yell back at your parents, could you? So you probably just took the scolding bravely, although you were madder than a hornet inside.

This is just the state of mind poltergeist children seem to be in *all the time*. They are very hostile, but they just can't seem to "let it all hang out," so to speak.

Now, I'll ask you another question: When you were younger and got mad, what did you do about it? Many children, when angry and frustrated, will start pounding their fists on walls, throwing things, slamming doors, and will just "work out" their anger that way. (I was a great object-thrower as a child, and, in fact, when I'm angry I still like to throw whatever is handy against some nearby wall.) Notice that this is exactly what the poltergeist does also. It, too, thumps on walls, throws things, and so forth. You see, the poltergeist carries out the very acts the poltergeist-child would *like to do,* but can't for one reason or another. Instead of throwing anything himself, the poltergeist-agent liberates some force from his mind which carries out these acts for him.Usually though, these people do not realize that they are actually responsible for the disturbances. They might, in all honesty, blame the pranks on some ghost or "evil spirit."

Of course, no one knows exactly what this mind-over-matter energy is. It is an energy totally mysterious and unknown to modern science. Nor do we know why only certain people become poltergeist-creators. The only thing we do know is that the poltergeist is the way in which some people unconsciously express anger. But at least that is a lot more than we know about most kinds of psychic phenomena.

6. ANIMAL GHOSTS AND HAUNTINGS

I've known Raymond Bayless ever since my high school days. He is a shrewd psychic investigator and over the years has taught me more about the ghost-hunting business than any other researcher I've ever known. We are still friends and colleagues, and since 1967 we have investigated scores of cases together.

I can still remember the very first time Raymond invited me to his house. That's when I met his wife, Marjorie, and their three beautiful—but very different—cats. First there was Devil, a huge black and white animal blessed with an immense tail, but cursed by a mean streak that often overcame his usual pleasant nature. The second of the Baylesses' cats was named Kitty, a pretty tiger-striped cat they had found abandoned one day out in the desert. Their third cat was simply named —Ann. She was the smallest, but the oldest, of the three.

I'll always remember meeting Raymond's cats that evening. That's the day I learned I was allergic to cat hair!

Over the years I got to know the Bayless cats very well. (I just didn't pet them very often.) Each had his or her own very individual personality and voice. For instance, Kitty would often let out a strange "meow" which sounded somewhat like a rusty gate creaking open, while Ann had a milder and softer voice. I also grew to appreciate the fact that Raymond and Marjorie probably loved their cats more than anything else in the world, so it deeply pained me as I watched the sorrow that overcame them as their cats grew old and sickly.

Between 1972 and 1976, all three of them had to be put
to sleep one by one. So I guess that's why I wasn't too
surprised when the Baylesses informed me that their
former pets had come back to "haunt" them after their
deaths. It all just seemed so natural.

Actually, the Baylesses experienced three separate
rashes of haunting-type phenomena in their Los Angeles
home during these years. As you might have guessed,
each group of incidents seemed directly related to the
death of each of their cats. The first occurred in March,
1972, shortly after Kitty passed on. The Baylesses encountered an even more impressive, but short-lived,
haunting in their house in February, 1975, right after
Ann had to be put to sleep; while a third mini-haunting
broke out after Devil's death. Of course, Raymond and
Marjorie wrote out detailed notes describing all of these
ghostly activities right at the time they occurred. So my
files on the Bayless hauntings are very complete.

Kitty (or K.K.—short for Kitty Kitty—as the Baylesses liked to call him) died on February 23, 1972. He
wasn't an old cat, but he had developed cancer. So the
Baylesses had him put to sleep by a veterinarian in order
to spare him the misery of a slow and painful death.
They buried him lovingly in their own backyard. The
Baylesses were extremely upset by their pet's death, but
were somewhat consoled when, a few weeks later, they
began to realize that Kitty was somehow still present in
the house and apparently trying to make his presence
known. The first sign that the cat had "come back" to
haunt the house came on March 10th. Raymond was
sleeping in the living room at the time.

"At approximately 5 or 6 o'clock in the morning,"
Raymond notes in his account of the haunting, "I was
awakened by a clear, obvious sound of a cat cry definitely from inside the house. Having cats, we are used to
waking up immediately to a cry or any unusual sound in
order to investigate to see if there is any problem. So my
waking up was quite normal. At first I thought it was

Ann, but then realized almost instantly that the cry was the unusual 'rusty gate' sound of Kitty. This odd-sounding cry was very peculiar to him, and, in fact, I have never heard another cat with this unusual voice."

Although taken by surprise, Raymond looked around and saw that his other two cats were right in the room with him. They were resting comfortably, so probably had not made the cry. And oddly, they took absolutely no notice of the phantom sound.

Raymond was, of course, both startled and puzzled by the incident and didn't quite know what to make of it. Later that night, though, he was in for an even greater surprise when Marjorie spontaneously told him that *she* had heard a very faint sound in the house that very evening which sounded to her like Kitty's voice. So Raymond wasn't alone in thinking that perhaps their former pet was somehow returning to them. When he spoke to me about the incident the next day on the phone, Raymond also added that he had not told his wife about his own experience until learning of hers. So when she heard the phantom cry that evening for herself, he added, she had no way of knowing that he had also heard an identical cry that morning. The fact that both Raymond and Marjorie heard the same sound, though totally independently of each other, is very evidential.

New phenomena broke out in the Bayless home the very next day, but this time Marjorie was the only witness.

It was midnight and Marjorie, who was having difficulty sleeping that night, was lying in bed fully awake when she heard what sounded like a small animal trotting about the room. She distinctly heard the familiar clicking sounds which always indicated that one of their cats was in the room and walking about the wood floors before sneaking into bed with them. Marjorie bolted upright in bed when she heard the sounds and tried to see what was causing the strange patter. Ann was already in bed right next to her, and she found Devil snoozing comfortably in the living room. So whatever had walked into the room was obviously quite invisible.

Was it Kitty? The Baylesses were beginning to think so, but this incident ended the two-day haunting.

Although this haunting consisted only of three incidents, it is an impressive case, nonetheless. In one respect, these phenomena almost make a certain amount of sense. At first, both Raymond and Marjorie heard the voice of the cat on the same day, although at different times. To me, it seems as though the ghostly visitor was trying to independently assure *both* Raymond and Marjorie of his presence. And then, the very next day, the phantom seemed to bid the Baylesses a last farewell by pacing around their bedroom. The only truly curious thing about the case is that neither Devil nor Ann reacted in any way to the phantom presence.

Ann, who lived through Kitty's death and "return," became a ghost herself three years later. Her return was no less remarkable. Like her little playmate, she too had to be put to sleep because of ill health and died on February 1, 1975. Raymond buried her in his backyard right next to Kitty's little grave. Unlike Kitty, though, it didn't take Ann any time at all to psychically visit her former masters.

At eleven o'clock that very night, Raymond was lying on the couch when he heard the distinct sound of a cat's cry, just as he had three years before. This incident startled him since both Devil and another cat he had adopted were sitting right in the room with him and hadn't uttered a sound. And just as during the previous haunting, neither responded in any way to the phantom cry.

"The cry was either Ann's voice or a sound outside the house which sounded exactly like her voice," Raymond said when he phoned me to report the incident. "I can't dismiss the possibility that it was her voice."

However, nothing more happened in the Bayless home until three weeks later, on the night of February

25th, when both Raymond and Marjorie witnessed another curious event which they immediately linked to Ann.

"While lying in bed at approximately 11:05," notes Raymond, "my wife and I heard a heavy, soft 'thump' on a dresser across the bedroom. We both located the source of the sound. It was loud and sounded exactly as though a large cat jumped on it in some way. At the time we both looked up but the room was too dark to see if a cat (we now had two) had jumped on its top."

Of course, Raymond got up and immediately checked around. He found both of his cats sleeping quite soundly in the living room, so they could not have produced the noise. This incident ended the haunting.

I find it very interesting that this phantom cat behaved almost exactly as Kitty's "ghost" had. At first, Raymond only heard her cry, and then he and his wife were disturbed by a loud movement in their bedroom. So this case looks just like a replay of their 1972 haunting. Likewise, it is also interesting to note that, as in the previous mini-haunting, the Baylesses' living cats did not react to the ghost in any way. They were either immune to the phenomena or simply realized that there was nothing to be alarmed at. This indicates to me that they may have realized that the disturbances were being caused by their former playmate. Since animals often react strangely in haunted houses (for instance refer back to the Cheltenham haunting recounted in Chapter 1), the fact that Raymond's cats never responded to any of these incidents is probably telling us something very important about the nature of these hauntings. Just *what*, though, I don't know.

Devil, the last of the Bayless cats, had to be put to sleep a year after Ann's death and it looks as though he too came back from death to pay his owners a last farewell. Although Raymond experienced nothing unusual during the months after Devil's passing, Marjorie thought she saw his apparition about a week after his burial. She was sitting alone in the living room that night, and was not doing anything in particular at the time, when she swore that for a single moment she saw "Devil" sitting on the cat pole they have in the living room. She only saw it flash in the corner of her eye, and when she looked right at the pole a moment later the apparition was gone. But what really impressed Marjorie was that she thought she also heard scratching sounds coming from the pole at the same time she glimpsed the ghost. The very next day, Marjorie was in her sewing room (which is located at the back of the house behind the kitchen) when she thought she heard a cry resembling Devil's voice. She couldn't locate the source of the sound, but it seemed to come from the kitchen.

Just what can we make of all this? Did the Bayless cats actually return as ghosts to haunt them? Or can there be some other explanation to account for these three outbreaks of psychic phenomena?

If people can come back as ghosts after their deaths, one could argue, then there's no reason why animals couldn't as well. After all, why should man have a monopoly on immortality if survival after death is a fact? If for instance a pet has had an especially strong link with its master or to the house in which it lived, it is very possible that it may somehow become "tied" there after death. However, remember that in Chapter 1 I said that ghosts are not necessarily spirits of the dead. They may be "memory pictures" or "energy forms" somehow psychically created by a person before or at the time of his passing. The same goes for animal apparitions and hauntings as well. In other words, we know just as little about animal ghosts as we do about human ones.

In trying to understand the Baylesses' experiences, we also have to take into account the existence of the poltergeist. As I explained in the previous chapter, during these "hauntings" it looks as though a living person is using his or her psychic powers to create the disturbances. There can be no doubt that living people can sometimes cause ghostly disturbances in their own homes. Therefore, we have to ask ourselves a very important question. Could the Baylesses have themselves produced, quite unconsciously, all the phenomena they experienced after their cats died? This is a definite possibility, although it would be a difficult theory to prove. However, it would be just as difficult to prove that the cats were actually causing the hauntings. In parapsychology, there is never an easy answer to any question.

Perhaps it is nothing more than a curious coincidence that Raymond once actually wrote a book entitled *Animal Ghosts*. This was long before he had any idea that he would eventually come face to face with the ghosts of his own three pets. He has long had a special interest in animal hauntings and believes that our dead pets do indeed survive death and can, on occasion, come back to haunt us. But, he suggests in his book, these hauntings may not be a result of the type of tragedy or misery which is so often linked to human ghosts. Our pets might haunt us, quite simply, because they wish to return and be with us.

At this point, I'll have to admit that I had a very unusual and ghostly experience myself when my beagle, Freddy, died in 1971. Although not exactly a case of an animal haunting, it was—in one sense—an encounter with an animal ghost. The incident occurred shortly after I had moved away from home and into my own apartment. Here's the whole story, which I have never told before. At the time, it just seemed too personal to share with very many people:

In one respect, Freddy had been "my" dog. I was the one who originally picked him out from a large litter years before when our family decided to adopt a puppy for my brother and me. I was only about seven or so at the time, and I grew up with Freddy as my pet. He was a large beagle, very cowardly, but also so good-natured that I can only recall one time when he ever growled at anyone. (Some villain was trying to take his bone away.)

Although I really loved Freddy, he was, to put it bluntly, spoiled rotten. For instance, one day my parents decided that he should sleep in the living room at night instead of in their bed as he had done for several years. Freddy didn't like the idea one bit! He made it quite plain, by crying all night, that he much preferred my parents' large and warm bed to the living room couch. So in order to train him to stay in the living room at night, my parents had to block off the room with a baby fence. This was a three-foot high gate which guarded the doorway and which prevented Freddy from roaming the house at night in search of more comfortable sleeping quarters. That was all very fine for my parents, but not for me. My bedroom was right next to the living room and every morning, right at daybreak, Freddy would get up and rattle the gate with his paw. This was to let me know that he was up and wanted to go outside. I always had to get up, let him out, and then creep back into bed. This was my morning routine for years.

When I moved into my own apartment, Freddy stayed at my parents' house where he had a big yard in which to romp around and another dog to keep him company. It seemed as though he would live forever. Then, in 1971, his health started to fail, slowly and painfully. In fact before he eventually had to be put to sleep, my parents had to rush him to the vet on two occasions. I was, of course, concerned about him, but for some reason it never dawned on me that Freddy was nearing death.

One morning, several weeks after Freddy had first become ill, and after I had moved away, I woke up very groggy. I was still half asleep when I heard what sounded like a gate rattling in the living room. I was so confused that at first I didn't realize where I was. I immediately thought I was still at home. Of course, I assumed the noise was just Freddy wanting to be let out. I even mumbled half-aloud, "OK, Freddy, I'm coming." Hardly had I said these words than I heard the sound of an animal clicking its feet on the wooden floor of my bedroom. (Compare this experience to that of the Baylesses after Kitty's death.) Again, I thought of Freddy. By this time, though, I was more fully awake and suddenly realized that I wasn't living at home any more. I shook my head a couple of times, in order to wake myself up a bit more, and then plopped back to sleep. I merely thought the strange noises were part of some dream.

Later that day, though, I learned that my parents had found Freddy very sick that morning and had taken him to the vet. The doctor worked on him all day trying to save the poor animal, but Freddy was beyond hope and had to be put to sleep that afternoon. I still carry his picture in my wallet.

I've described this incident in depth because it illustrates how very hard it sometimes is to figure out what a "ghost" actually is. To begin with, there was no baby fence in my apartment, so the ghostly sounds which I so definitely heard were not genuine physical noises. They were illusions. And what about the footsteps I heard? Did Freddy's ghost come to bid me a last farewell? This could hardly be the case, since the dog was still alive at the time I had my experiences. So, while something very ghostly happened to me that day, there is practically no chance that my dog's "spirit" was in any way actually present in my apartment. But how can we explain these unusual events? Certainly the fact that I had these unusual experiences the very day Freddy died is more than coincidental. So here's how I would explain this case. Note how this explanation can also account for many other ghosts—animal and human—as well.

In the previous chapter, I showed that we can use PK

without even knowing it. We probably use ESP—extrasensory perception—the same way. ESP may work somewhat like radar, although this is only a very rough comparison. Nevertheless, a great deal of evidence exists which indicates that our minds are constantly using ESP to "scan" about all the time. However, it is only when our ESP latches onto something very important—such as when someone we love has been killed or injured in an accident miles away—that we have a *conscious* ESP experience. So while we are probably receiving ESP impressions all the time, we rarely notice them unless they are very strong. Sometimes, however, we will *respond* to an ESP message even though we have no idea that our behavior is being guided psychically. Have you ever had the following experience?

You might be walking down the street, just thinking how you would like to see an old school friend you haven't seen in a long time. You might then get a sudden urge to turn around and walk back the other way, only to bump into that very person only moments later. This could be just a wild coincidence. That's certainly true enough. But it is also possible that you were using ESP without knowing it. Somehow you knew, though not consciously, that in order to see your friend you had to turn around and walk the other way. Many odd coincidences are probably due to this very sort of ESP.

Now, however, let's apply all this to my experience.

It is very likely that, through just such an ESP "scanning process," I learned that my dog was dying. My mind might then have produced a series of illusions—such as my hearing the gate rattle and the footsteps—in order to make sure I got the message. In other words, these noises were not "real" sounds, but ESP impressions, although I didn't realize it at the time. It is very likely that many ghosts are actually ESP "visions" and not spirits of the dead. For example, take a look at the following case:

Lucian Landau is a businessman now living on the

Isle of Man, a scenic island located off the coast of England. He's both a scientist and inventor, and has designed a number of devices used in the rubber and plastic industries. He's hardly what you would call a "kook." He's also a natural-born psychic and has written on such topics as dowsing (also called "water-witching") and clairvoyance. However, one of Mr. Landau's most unusual experiences occurred one night when he encountered a ghostly dog. The entire case is recounted by Andrew MacKenzie, whose psychic investigations were mentioned in Chapter 1, in his book *The Unexplained*.

The incident occurred on December 6, 1955 when Landau was visiting a friend of his, Mr. Constantin Antoniades, in Geneva, Switzerland during a business trip. His host had met him at the airport upon his arrival and they had almost immediately gone together to inspect some factories. It had been a long day, and when evening came Landau was eager to retire to his room and go to sleep. He didn't realize that he was about to have a very unusual ghostly encounter.

Sometime later that night, Landau woke up with a start and with the feeling that someone had entered the room. On turning around, he saw an odd pool of light. As he watched the shimmering mass with growing interest, an apparition which resembled his host's wife gradually appeared alongside a large phantom Alsatian dog. The dog was brown, not black like so many Alsatians. As he watched in amazement, the figure whispered, "Tell him," and disappeared.

The next morning Landau told his host about his strange adventure. Mr. Antoniades was surprised when his guest mentioned the Alsatian and readily admitted that his wife had owned such a dog before her death, but that it had been given away. The dog, he said, *had* been brown, not black.

"When my wife became ill," he told Landau, "I found it too difficult to look after and had to give him away.

He is in some kennel some sixty miles from here."

Landau was puzzled, since it seemed to him that the dog must be dead. Why else, he thought, should he have seen it? To resolve the matter, he and Mr. Antoniades called the kennel and discovered that, indeed, the dog had been destroyed only a few days earlier.

There are two ways we can explain this case. On one hand, while staying in Mr. Antoniades' house Landau may have psychically learned about his host's wife and her dog unconsciously. His mind may then have created a vision of them—just as my mind made me think I was hearing things the day Freddy died. So, according to this theory, these two ghosts weren't real spirits at all. They were "ESP visions." On the other hand, though, it is also possible that the apparitions really were the surviving spirits of his host's wife and her dog. Perhaps she had returned to let her husband know that they had been reunited. This might explain why Landau heard the apparition say, "Tell him." Since Landau is a gifted psychic, the ghosts may have found it easier to appear to him than directly to Mr. Antoniades.

You can take your pick between these theories. Each one fits the facts. It's up to each of you to decide for yourself which theory seems more likely. However, it is also very important to listen to what people who have had these types of experiences say about them. So in October, 1977 I wrote directly to Mr. Landau and asked him what *he* thought about his experience. Here's what he wrote back:

As you rightly point out, to anyone not directly involved, two explanations of my experience in the house of Mr. Antoniades are possible. However, during the years 1953-1958 when I was intensely engaged in the subject, I found I could tell the difference between when I was acquiring information by ESP and when I was observing actual "spirit" entities. In the first case, people and animals appeared just like pic-

tures. They neither moved nor made any sounds. In
the second, they seemed alive, often spoke, or made
other sounds. Mrs. Antoniades certainly appeared
alive and spoke to me. Her dog likewise looked like a
live dog, not like an image of one. I think that the
evidence for survival after death is overwhelming.
Now, why should this not apply to animals?

The experiences of Raymond Bayless, Lucian Landau, and my own may not strike you as true hauntings in
the more conventional sense. Remember, I define a
haunting as "any place, including a house, where psychic phenomena occur over and over again and over a
long period of time." This definition doesn't quite fit
Mr. Landau's experience or mine. Even the three mini-
hauntings which the Baylesses encountered were not really full-fledged hauntings. After all, none of them lasted
any longer than a couple of days or just a few weeks. But
don't let this fool you. Just as with more conventional
ghosts, animals can haunt their former homes for years.
So before concluding this chapter, let's at least take a
look at one such case. In this psychic drama, a ghostly
Great Dane played the starring role.

The key incidents in this unusual story took place in
1926, when Mrs. Helen Daniels, her little daughter Betty, and her five-year-old son moved into a large house
on an unnamed island off the English coast. At the time,
the Danielses had just returned from China and had
rented the house from a close family friend. Besides the
family members, the children's nurse and several English servants also lived there. The haunting started only
a day after the Danielses moved in.

"Our first night in the house was serene," wrote Mrs.
Daniels in her report on the haunting, "but the second
night, Betty, who was sleeping alone, began to scream
with fright about fifteen minutes after Nai-nai, her Chi-
nese nurse, had put her to bed. Nai-nai and I asked her
if she had had a nightmare but she insisted that she had

been awake and that a big black dog had come and put his head on the edge of her crib. She was terrified and trembled with fright. She didn't fall asleep until we had looked all around and had assured her that there was no big dog in the house."

Mrs. Daniels was very surprised by her daughter's reaction to the dog since never before had she even shown any fear of them. Quite to the contrary, she liked dogs and had already made friends with a little spaniel named Flossie who often hung around the house. However, there was something about *this* dog that was very frightening to the little girl. Mrs. Daniels continues:

> The next day we explained to Betty that no dog could have entered her room and she apparently believed us and forgot the matter. That night Nai-nai was sitting in the day nursery near the door of Betty's room after she had been put to bed when she began to shriek again. When Nai-nai went in to her, she was absolutely overwrought with terror. She said that the same big dog had come and put his head on her bed. She described the animal exactly as she had the night before.
>
> I still attributed the whole thing to either imagination or a nightmare, but Nai-nai, who was a wise old Chinese and who had looked after Betty since her birth and consequently knew her character very intimately, insisted that the child had "seen something." She furthermore insisted that, whatever the explanation, it was bad for her to be frightened in that way. Thereafter she kept a night light in Betty's room and sat with her for some time after she went to sleep. Betty slept quietly after that and the trouble never re-occurred.

The solution to the mystery only came a week later when Mrs. Daniels's godmother, who owned the house, came to visit and learned about Betty's experiences. She immediately asked to speak with the girl. However, she asked her questions very carefully so that the child had no way of knowing what answers she expected in return.

"What sort of dog was it, Betty?" asked the elderly woman.

"A big dog," answered Betty, "a very big dog."

"What were the ears like?" continued Mrs. Daniels's godmother.

"They stood up like this, not like Flossie's ears," came the reply.

The elderly woman obviously realized that something was up, and also made it quite apparent that she knew more than she was telling either Betty or her mother.

"Was he black like my dress, Betty, or brown like the furniture here?" she finally asked.

"He was black, not brown like Flossie," answered Betty who was then scooted off to bed.

After Betty had left the room, the woman told Mrs. Daniels the whole story about the island's phantom dog. The previous owners of the island, she said, had owned a huge black Great Dane which was never penned up and had the run of the whole island. He served as both pet and guard dog, but one night he was beaten to death by one of the island residents. No one knew who killed the dog, but it was a savage act. Afterwards, its ghost started to appear near the house and several servants and workers had in fact seen it over the years. Many of the islanders knew about the ghost, and it was something of a local legend.

Mrs. Daniels was intrigued by the story, so she immediately tried to find out if someone could have told the tale to Betty. If so, this might have frightened her into having nightmares. However Betty's nurse had never heard the story and the girl could not have had any contact whatsoever with the islanders. She had only been on the island for a couple of days and was only two and a half years old. Apparently, the child really had seen the ghost.

By no means is this the end to this strange story. In 1929, Mrs. Daniels's godmother decided to move back to the island herself for the summer and brought a new maid along with her. The maid had never lived on the island before and knew nothing of its history. One day, though, she complained to her mistress that she had seen a huge black dog in the house!

A much sadder and almost heartbreaking account of a ghostly dog was reported in 1950 to the American Society for Psychical Research by Mrs. W.E. Dickson. This case is impressive because of the large number of witnesses to the short-lived haunting. Earlier, I suggested that certain "ghosts" are probably ESP-projected impressions produced by the onlookers themselves. However, this theory certainly can't explain this case, which was reported in the October, 1952 issue of the *Journal* of the A.S.P.R. Mrs. Dickson reported:

I have had many psychic experiences since childhood but perhaps the most interesting has to do with our dog "Butch," who died exactly one year ago at the age of five years. Butch lived with us in our home and was highly regarded as a member of our family. We loved him dearly and he returned our love.

He died about noon on Tuesday, March 29, 1949. Tuesday night I heard him whining and crying all night long. I wasn't going to tell my husband because I didn't think that he would believe me. However, the next morning he said to me, "I don't know if you will believe this, but I heard Butch crying all night." We decided not to say anything about this to anyone, but changed our minds when one of our neighbors (who was with us when Butch was dying) came over and said "Don't know whether to tell you this or not, but last night [Tuesday] I dreamed that I heard Butch crying and went to the door, opened it, and there he was." The only difference in our experiences was that we were wide awake when we heard Butch, and our friend was dreaming.

For about two months after Butch's death I heard him crying for me, and my husband swears that he heard him bark loudly at the back door to be let in.

Had the neighbor telepathically "picked up" the Dicksons' experiences? Or had he heard the cries while sleeping which caused him to dream about the dog? These are questions nobody can answer. But at least this ghostly dog was so material that many people could hear him. The case also proves that some ghosts—even animal ones—can be very, very real.

Is this photograph genuine or a hoax? According to the December 31, 1955 issue of the *Baltimore Sun*, the picture was snapped aboard the U.S.S. Constellation by an executive officer at Fort McHenry. *Photo from the files of Fate Magazine.*

This "ghost-photograph" was taken in a haunted house in England in the 1930's, by the occupant of the house who only saw a "curious light" at the time.

The famous "Brown Lady" of Raynham Hall, as photographed by Mr. Indre Shira on September 19, 1936. (See text, chapter 1.) *Photo from the files of Fate Magazine.*

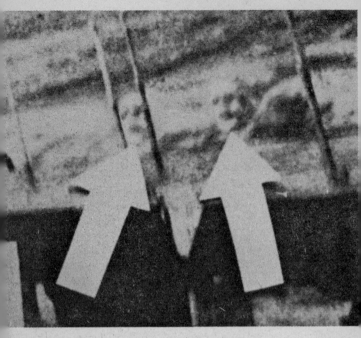

This S.S. Watertown photograph was taken in 1924 and shows the faces of two seamen who died aboard ship and who continue to follow it on ocean voyages. (See text, chapter 1.) *Photo from the files of Fate Magazine.*

In 1948, this "ghost" was photographed by a Los Angeles woman while taking a snapshot of her front yard. Note the face behind the tree and the odd "cord" leading to it. The three lights in the tree are reflections.

This ghostly picture was given to the author by a woman who claimed that it was taken by her son during World War II inside a cathedral in Algeria. Real or fake? What do you think?

Two views of Borley Rectory. (See text, chapter 2.) *Printed with the permission of George Harrap & Co., Ltd.*

Marianne

Marianne

Marianne
Please hel
get

Marianne

I CANNOT UNDERSTAND
TELL ME MORE

Marianne.

I STILL CANNOT UNDERSTAND
PLEASE TELL ME MORE.

Investigators were able to photograph this light fixture, in the Rosenheim law office, swing by itself. (See text, chapter 5.) *Reprinted with the permission of Paul Elek, Ltd.*

◄ Etchings found on the walls of Borley Rectory. (See text, chapter 2.) The block letters were written by the Foysters as they tried to encourage the Borley ghosts to communicate further. *Printed with permission of George Harrap & Co., Ltd.*

Annemarie Schnabel, around whom the Rosenheim poltergeist centered, is standing under the light fixture which would often swing by itself in her presence. (See text, chapter 5.) *Reprinted with the permission of Paul Elek, Ltd.*

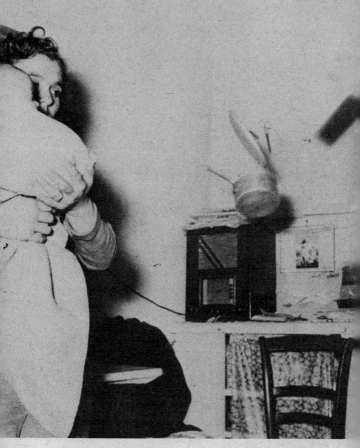

This photograph, taken in France in 1955 shows a poltergeist in action. The photographers were doing a story on the case when objects started moving by themselves.

1.

2.

3.

The three cats that came back to haunt
Mr. and Mrs. Raymond Bayless: 1) Kitty,
2) Ann, 3) Devil. (See text, chapter 6.)

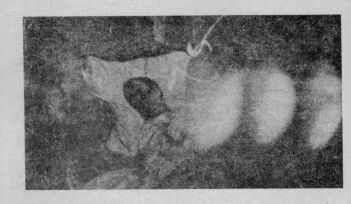

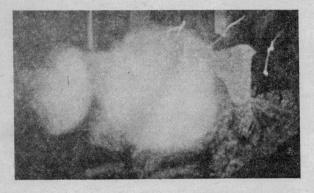

Dr. Baraduc's photographs of the "psychic forms" given off by the body of his wife after death. Could this be the stuff of which ghosts are made? (See text, chapter 7.)

7. WHAT MAKES A HOUSE HAUNTED?

Perhaps I should begin this chapter by saying that no one really knows what makes a haunted house. There are so many types of hauntings—human ghosts, animal hauntings, evil presences, and so on—that no one working in parapsychology has of yet ever come up with one general theory which can explain all of them. Any comprehensive theory would have to account for a huge variety of phenomena. It would have to account for the ghosts of both men and animals so often seen in haunted houses; phantom noises; strange odors; object movements; and many other psychic phenomena. Such a theory would also have to explain why some hauntings seem related to past tragedies which once took place in the house or building, while others are not. Developing such a theory is no easy matter, and few parapsychologists agree about what underlying force causes a house to become haunted.

However, this is not to say that parapsychologists have given up all hope that we might eventually discover what force actually produces the various phenomena which occur in these mysterious place, and why a house becomes haunted in the first place. Over the past hundred years or so, many parapsychologists have suggested theories about haunted houses and in this chapter we'll take a look at some of them. Now some of these explanations are pretty complicated. But if you can't quite understand one or two of them, don't worry. Many parapsychologists don't either!

As I implied above, just about every ghost-hunter I

know has his own ideas about what force is working its magic spell in these places. However very few experts really believe that a ghost is literally the "spirit" body of a once living person who, through some horrible tragedy, has become trapped in a house. This popular belief has never been taken too seriously by parapsychologists. This is not to say that psychical researchers necessarily reject the possibility that some hauntings are caused by the activities of the dead. Most professionals just don't believe that ghosts are *themselves* the actual forms of the dead. This explanation just doesn't seem to make much sense. Just look at the cases summarized in this book. In many of the hauntings I've described, no evidence was ever found which indicated that the houses in question had ever been the scene of past tragedy or violence. Futhermore, many hauntings take place in very modern buildings. And in some haunted houses, there is no evidence at all that *any* personality, much less that of a deceased person, is actually active there. Take a look at the house in which I lived, for instance. When I traced its background, I learned that no one had ever died there. Indeed, the house had been a wedding chapel at one time. But there was no history of violence of any sort associated with it. And when I got to know the previous owners of the house, they told me that they had never encountered anything unusual in the place at all. Yet the house was definitely haunted. But by whom? I could never discover the answer to that gnawing question, probably because there wasn't any. Looking back on the case today, it seems to me more likely that the house was haunted by a "force," or by some bizarre psychic energy which constantly built up and then discharged itself, than by a spirit presence.

To be sure, there *are* cases on record in which houses have become haunted after having been the scene of some violence or tragedy. And the ghosts which appear in these places very often resemble the unfortunate victims of these melodramas. But even in these cases, there is little evidence that the apparitions which eventually appeared in these houses are literally the spirits of the dead. For one thing, they rarely show any intelligence. They act more like mechanical dolls than self-aware entities. Often they just seem to pace about as though in trance, and only rarely do they take any notice of anyone living in the house. Secondly, they often appear dressed in clothes! So we have to ask ourselves the embarrassing question: If ghosts are real beings, where do their ghostly garments come from? From what ethereal substance are they made? Third, ghosts often appear holding canes, wearing glasses, or carrying candles, and so on. Yet these objects seem to be just as non-material as the phantoms holding them. In other words, it looks as though most ghosts are somehow *images,* like a TV picture or a daydream, and are not really physical objects. This explains the facts a lot better than believing that they are actually spirits of the dead. Nonetheless, it is very true that sometimes ghosts can influence our physical world. They have been known to open doors, throw things, and even push people. Occasionally, a ghost is seen collectively, as though every one in its presence is seeing a very real being. They have even been seen reflected in mirrors. So one might say that a ghost is a non-material object (or image), but that it possesses some sort of physical force. In short, a ghost is both real and unreal at the same time. So now you know why they are so hard to study, explain, or understand!

Now let's turn to hauntings in general. As pointed out previously, many theories have been proposed to account for these eerie places. Some of them are rather naive, and a few are downright preposterous. Others are more complicated and mind-boggling. But let's examine all of them anyway, and as unbiasedly as possible.

Some of the very first psychical researchers tried to argue that *true* haunted houses and ghosts really don't exist at all. Instead, they said, these phenomena are caused by telepathy among the living. Here, in simple form, is how these investigators thought a house became "haunted":

Let's say you move into a house in a new neighborhood. You don't know anything about the background of the house but, unknown to you, a large family of mice live quite comfortably in your cellar. So one night you wake up and start hearing strange thumping sounds coming from under the floor. Since you don't know what is actually causing the noises, you jump to the wrong conclusion and begin to think that the house is haunted. Of course, it isn't, but that's not the point. What is important is that you *think* the house is haunted. In fact, you get very wrapped up in the idea. You might begin to misinterpret any old creak or thump as something supernatural. And any odd reflection or shadow in the house might begin to look like a genuine ghost. This all just might make you believe even more that you are living in a haunted house.

So now we have a haunted house with all the trappings: footsteps, poundings, ghosts, etc. At this point in the game, other members of your family might start "picking up" your thoughts by telepathy. Then *they* might automatically start seeing ghosts or hearing sounds. These, though, are only telepathic illusions similar to the ones I experienced when my pet beagle was dying. Soon everyone in your family thinks the house is haunted because you are all continually picking up each other's thoughts.

Now, let's go on with this idea even further. Let's say that eventually you and your family sell the house to someone else and move. This new family might start psychically responding to your thoughts or emotions, which might still be lingering in the house, and they too might start experiencing everything you thought you were experiencing. Zap! One haunted house to order!

Of course, we now know that this theory cannot account for many of the phenomena that are often produced in haunted houses at all, but many years ago it was taken quite seriously. For instance, this theory cannot explain why ghosts so often resemble the previous tenants of the houses they haunt. Just look back to the Cheltenham ghost which was discussed in Chapter 2. Only after having seen the ghost on several occasions did Rose Despard discover that the figure looked very much like Mrs. Imogene Swinhoe, who had lived in the house several years earlier. Nor does the "telepathy" theory account for the fact that sometimes physical objects, such as furniture, will move about by themselves in haunted places. No telepathic fantasy can do that.

It is possible, though, that a few hauntings do in fact come into existence by just this process. Not all or even many, mind you, but perhaps a few. For example, back in 1966 Dr. Gertrude Schmeidler, a psychologist at the City College of the City University of New York, reported just such a probable case to the American Society for Psychical Research.

One day, it seems, a friend of Dr. Schmeidler's casually mentioned that she thought her New York home was haunted. She had lived in the house since 1961, she said, and over the last two and a half years she had gradually become aware of some invisible "presence" lurking about. She could not rid herself of the feeling. She never saw the ghost, or anything like it. She just "felt" that some invisible being was sharing the house with her and her family, and could feel this presence particularly strongly in certain rooms of the three-story dwelling. Her daughter, too, she admitted to Dr. Schmeidler, could feel this presence on occasion, often in the same areas of the house. And only recently, she finally added, her teenage son had become sensitive to it also. Her husband seemed immune to the ghost, though.

Dr. Schmeidler was interested enough by the report to organize a full investigation of the house. First, she drew up a floorplan of the house and had each of the family members independently check off where they thought the ghost's presence was the strongest. Then she rounded up eleven volunteers who all felt that they were psychic and, one by one, had them visit the house while the family was away. They too were given the floor plan and asked to check off any location where they felt that the ghost was particularly active.

When the experiment was over, Dr. Schmeidler discovered that many of her subjects independently agreed that a ghost was really present in the house and somehow linked to two specific rooms. Interestingly enough, these were the same two rooms in which the family members had also experienced the presence so forcefully.

Now this is just the type of case which can be easily explained by the "telepathy among the living" theory. It seems to me quite possible that Dr. Schmeidler's friend only imagined the ghost. As she became more concerned and frightened, though, her daughter might have begun picking up her fears by telepathy. This could easily have caused the daughter to become sensitive to this "presence" too, although her experience was probably only a telepathic illusion. Eventually, the son might have joined into this telepathic rapport. The fact that so many of Dr. Schmeidler's psychic friends also felt the ghost's presence in the house doesn't surprise me either. Perhaps they were just telepathically receiving this information from the family members.

Another type of "telepathic" theory was also proposed by some of the first parapsychologists. They suggested that some houses are in fact "haunted" by the *memories* of someone who had once lived there—memories which are still lingering about. People coming into contact with such a house, they reasoned, might then telepathically tap these memories and start vividly experiencing them as their own; that is, by "seeing" the ghosts of people who had once lived there or by hearing the sounds of past events. These phenomena, this theory goes on to say, are not real. Again, they are only telepathic illusions, but in this case the telepathy is between the living and the dead!

However, even this theory still does not explain why some ghosts can pick up books or turn doorknobs. It certainly cannot explain the following case, which was originally reported just a few years ago to the Institute of Psychophysical Research in Great Britain. The reporter was a young Englishman who, at the time of his experience was a child, visiting a friend with his parents. He had no idea he was staying in a haunted house, but that didn't keep him from running into the ghost face-to-face . . . a ghost so solid that it could even open a window blind:

I slept alone in a back bedroom and woke up suddenly one bright, windy, moonlit night at about 10.30 p.m. with the feeling that there was someone in the room. By the window, and clearly visible in the moonlight, there was a woman in a white nightdress, and I can still recall a double frilled yoke over the shoulders and a frilled collar.

She was holding the cream roller blind away from the curtains and the window, looking down into the yard of the house next door. After watching her for a while, I said, "Mother, what are you looking at?" but there was no reply. The question was repeated and the figure at the window turned to look at me and I was surprised to realise that it was not my mother.

At the same moment the figure gave the blind the sharp downward tug necessary to release it and it shot up to the roller with a crack like a shot.

I screamed twice for my father and disappeared under the bedclothes and he and my mother, fully dressed of course, ran upstairs from the room where they had both been reading. The incident, of course, was treated as a dream or nightmare but I would never sleep in that room again.

I found out months later that my 'dream' had caused quite a bit of interest amongst friends of the family, one of whom knew the owner of the house. We were told that he had married for the second time, a younger woman of whom he was very fond. She had died in that room of "Spanish flu", as it was referred to then, about a year before, and my description of her face, hair style and height bore some resemblance to her . . .

There were white lace curtains in a squared pattern at the window, which was partly open. There was a stiff breeze and moonlight and perhaps the wind had caused the blind to flap and release itself but I was aware during the incident of complete silence and of no movement for quite a time until the figure turned and the blind shot up . . . the blind which was always pulled down was up when my parents came into the room.

Obviously then, ghosts and hauntings are not due purely to telepathy, no matter how far we stretch the idea. And the theory that telepathy between the dead and the living can occur on rare occasions tells us just as little about haunted houses as does the idea that these places are caused by telepathy among the living. Cases such as the one cited above indicate that ghosts can become at least semiphysical objects. While most of them are no doubt merely images, it is also true that these images can either generate a physical force or can solidify into partially physical beings. It also seems likely that some partially physical psychic *force* is at work in many haunted houses. So, could it be that somehow the "atmosphere" of some houses, or their very walls, are somehow able to generate psychic forces? This is just the question many psychical researchers have begun to ask themselves. In other words, does a mind—living or dead—cause a haunting? Or does the building itself generate the phenomena?

The next two theories I would like to present both attempt to argue that physical matter—such as a house —can itself generate psychic impressions and forces, and that these forces can produce hauntings. In other words, these theories state that nothing *in* the house makes it haunted. Instead, certain houses can produce the phenomena on their very own! This may strike you as a strange concept, but it really isn't. Just take a look at the following facts:

Several years ago I tested a young woman named Mrs. S. who was gifted with a fascinating psychic ability. She could simply hold a small object in her hand, such as a ring or wallet, and then psychically describe its owner and even tell you all about the history of the object. She might, for example, describe its previous owners or the town in which it was made. This ability is called "psychometry," which roughly means "measure of the soul" in Greek. Psychometry can be defined as "the art of gaining ESP impressions from physical objects by merely touching them." Many psychics have this ability, and are called "psychometrists."

To be sure, many parapsychologists do not believe that psychometrists actually gain ESP impressions directly from the objects they handle. They argue that, more likely, the psychics are really only using these objects to help them read the minds of their present owners. I once saw a psychic correctly tell a friend of mine that he loved tapioca pudding just by holding his ring. It is highly likely that the psychic picked up this piece of information right from my friend's mind and not from the ring itself. However, this theory cannot explain all cases of psychometry. There is one experiment on record, which was reported years ago, during which a psychic was handed some clothing taken from a murdered man. The psychic was able to describe the murderer in detail. This could hardly have been accomplished through telepathy. Likewise, I know of another case in which a psychometrist touched a small stone and gave a perfect description of the town from which it came, although no one present knew from where the rock had originally come.

In these instances, it looks as though the psychics were actually gaining their impressions directly from the objects they touched. This discovery has led some parapsychologists to believe that physical objects might carry with them "psychic traces" they have picked up from their past owners. Physical objects might act just like miniature psychic tape-recorders and cameras. Now, I own a piece of porcelain that has been handed down through my family for three generations. It is very likely that somehow my grandmother, my mother, and I—by handling this piece—have all saturated it with psychic impressions about ourselves. A psychic might be able to tell me all about my relatives just by touching it and thereby coming into contact with these impressions.

Back in the 1880s, Mrs. Eleanor Sidgwick, who was a famous educator of her day and also one of Great Britain's leading authorities on psychic phenomena, suggested that a similar psychic process might account for the experiences many people have in so-called haunted houses. She proposed that perhaps a house "absorbs" psychic impressions from the people who have lived there. A house may capture whole scenes of past events just as though some cosmic movie camera were recording everything that had gone on there for years upon years. She further theorized that these impressions may become permanently attached to a house. This build-up of psychic influences just might cause the house to eventually become haunted. If, for instance, a person who is sensitive to psychic impressions enters a house where these influences are particularly strong, he or she might start to psychically react to them. These people might then start seeing visions of the people who lived there ("ghosts") or hearing sounds that were once produced there (footsteps, thumping noises, and so on).

There is a lot of evidence on hand which tends to support Mrs. Sidgwick's theory. For one thing, it explains why ghosts are sometimes seen by one person in a house, but will remain quite invisible to others. The Cheltenham ghost is a good case in point. Rose Despard and her sister could see the ghost, but their father never could. So perhaps they were more sensitive to these lingering impressions than their father was. Mrs. Sidgwick's theory can also explain why hauntings sometimes "skip" tenants. Perhaps these people or families are, likewise, just not psychic enough to make contact with these mysterious influences.

However, Mrs. Sidgwick's theory cannot explain many other puzzles we run into as we study haunted houses. Why is it, you might ask, that three independent visitors to a haunted house might all see or experience the exact same things? This fact puts a plug in Mrs. Sidgwick's theory. If a house can become haunted by all the influences it has collected over the years, why should different people all respond to the *exact same* impressions? Why wouldn't they react to different ones? For instance, why did the Despard sisters always see the ghost of Imogene Swinhoe? Why wasn't the ghost of *Mr.* Swinhoe ever seen? Likewise, this theory cannot explain how ghosts can move objects, open doors, or thump beds at night. Also, the psychometric theory does not explain why *every* house isn't haunted. If it is true that a house can somehow collect psychic impressions from its tenants, how come only certain buildings do in fact become haunted?

There is only one possible way of getting around this last problem, though. Perhaps only certain events or memories can become psychically registered on a house or building. So maybe this is why so many (but not all) haunted houses have a history of death or tragedy. Perhaps such an emotional event as a murder or accidental death sets up just the right psychic conditions which allow it, and no other impressions, to become attached to the house. If you throw a dart at a board without much force, it may well fail to puncture it and stick there. You have to throw it hard in order to make it lock in place. The same thing may apply to a house. Maybe only strong or violent scenes can "stick."

Mrs. Sidgwick's basic theory was revised many years later, taking the above argument somewhat into account, by Professor H.H. Price of Oxford University in a lecture he gave to the Society for Psychical Research on the subject in 1939. He calls his idea the "psychic ether" theory. He believes that all space is saturated by an all-filling semiphysical substance called "psychic ether." It exists in the same space as our air. You might call the psychic ether a sort of "psychic fourth dimension." Of course we can't see it, just as we cannot see air. But this ether is ever-present and very sensitive to psychic impressions. Price suggested that the psychic ether within a house might act something like a movie film. Past and present events taking place there are being continually registered on it. However, he goes on to say that when something very emotionally powerful happens in a house, this event might register so strongly that it literally blocks out everything else recorded on the ether. Every time a human mind comes in contact with such a house, he argues, this scene may become reactivated and replay itself over and over. In other words, our minds act like a sort of movie projector while the house acts as both the screen and film. In one respect, Price is saying that ghosts are like holograms. (A hologram is a three-dimensional image made from light. It has no substance of its own, so it doesn't really exist in physical space. You can even walk right through one. It's like a 3-D T.V. picture.) The reason why all houses aren't haunted, Price believes, is simply because it is only on rare occasions when one certain series of impressions on the ether of a house dominate the others. In a normal house, these impressions are so weak and jumbled up that our minds just block them out altogether.

Price also suggests that this "psychic ether" might on occasion become a physical force with the power to even move household furniture, open doors, and so forth. So, simply stated, Price believes that a house is haunted by the memories of the people who once lived there, and not by their "spirits."

Another psychical researcher, Ernesto Bozzano, whose views and research on haunted houses were mentioned in Chapter 1, did not believe that either Mrs. Sidgwick's or Professor Price's theories could account for all the various phenomena which have been reported by people who have lived in these houses. He felt that in the course of a haunting, the *mind* of a dead person is actually somehow *actively present* in the affected building. He further felt that this intelligence masterminds the haunting and produces all the phenomena we so often associate with these places. In his book on the subject, *Dei Fenomeni d'Infestazione* (first published in 1919), the Italian investigator cited five major reasons why he felt that only his "spiritistic" theory could explain everything we know about hauntings. Remember, Bozzano only came to these conclusions after having studied hundreds of cases:

1) Sometimes ghosts of the dead appear in houses in which they had not died, nor ever lived!

(2) No other theory can explain the physical phenomena, such as raps and object movements, so often produced in haunted houses.

(3) According to Price's and Sidgwick's theories, any house in which dramatic events ever took place should become haunted. But they don't.

(4) The spiritistic theory explains the intermittent nature of some hauntings.

(5) Sometimes a haunting will cease after some act is carried out on behalf of the ghost, or according to its instructions. For example, occasionally a haunting will halt after a *Requiem* (a mass for the dead) is said

in the house. In several other cases Bozzano cited, hauntings have suddenly stopped after bones were discovered in secret graves or entombed in old walls, and were given proper burial.

Nonetheless, Bozzano did not believe that ghosts were actually the spirit forms of the dead walking about. He suggested instead that anyone living in a haunted house might come into contact with the "mind" of a dead person which has somehow become trapped there. This independent mind might then telepathically cause this person to see its form, and cause objects to move about, etc. If you recall, I said at the beginning of this book that sometimes it seems as though ghosts can actually choose to whom they wish to appear. This observation is very consistent with Bozzano's views.

Of course, one could easily extend any of these theories. For instance, maybe a person who undergoes a tragic death might somehow project some sort of "psychic energy-form" of himself composed of the same type of "energy" which comes into play during PK displays. Just take a look at what the poltergeist can do! Perhaps the energy which we use to create these violent disturbances can, on occasion, survive our own deaths. This "energy" might then take on a life of its own and become a ghost with the power to move objects around, turn into a visible apparition, and so on. I'm rather drawn to this theory for the simple reason that living people sometimes become ghosts! I'm not referring to the poltergeist when I say this. But every once in awhile you will run into a conventional haunted house in which the ghost turns out to be a living person.

For example, the following case (which is drawn from the S.P.R.'s files) is an unusual one, to say the least. It is thoroughly described by B. Abdy Collins in his book *The Cheltenham Ghost:*

In October, 1886 a caller at the house of Dr. E. saw seated on a settee "with her back to her," a young

lady in a brown dress with a broad lace collar. Her
hair was reddish gold and she seemed to be reading.
The visitor talked for some time to Mrs. E. and another visitor, a man. When he left, she looked round
and the lady was gone. Mrs. E. had seen no one and
was a little alarmed. A year later the same figure was
seen twice at an interval of a week by a guest staying
in the house and by a servant. The guest Mrs. R. lying
in bed saw "her" enter the room, walk up to the
cheval glass and without a word begin to take down
her hair. Mrs. R. thinking it was a real woman, got
out of bed and laid her hand on her shoulder, only to
find it pass through empty air and to find herself
looking in the glass. The servant saw the figure walk
into the dining-room and following it found no one
there. In August, 1888, Mrs. E.'s son arrived from
Australia with his wife, who had been married to him
in Sydney and had never been seen by the family or
their friends before. She was not recognized at once,
as she had been ill and had her hair cut off, but later
when she revisited her mother-in-law, she came down
to dinner in a brown tea-gown with a lace collar and
was at once recognised by both Mrs. R. and the maid
as "the brown lady." The daughter-in-law herself was
not told of these incidents, but she told her mother
that while she was ill in Australia she used to try and
picture to herself the home her husband used to describe to her, but she does not seem on arrival to have
recognised any particular room.

This weird case suggests that all of us have the ability
to project ghosts of ourselves. At death, might not some
of us permanently project these forms into the homes in
which we have lived or visited?

Something just like this recently happened to me. In
August, 1977 I flew to New York from my home in Los
Angeles and left my house in the hands of a friend,
whom I'll simply call Dave. I was gone for three weeks,
but while away I started having odd sensations in the

evenings as I relaxed in my New York apartment. Sometimes I felt as though some force were being drawn from me when I lay down. Ultimately, I started having very vivid dreams of being back in my house. Usually I found myself walking up and down the hallway which enters into all of the bedrooms of my home. Then, after the evening of August 22nd, these sensations and dreams abruptly stopped.

.When I arrived back home a week later, I was faced with a very astonished friend. Within an hour of my return, Dave excitedly told me that all sorts of odd things had been happening in the house beginning on the very day I left. In the evenings he had heard low moaning sounds, and raps, and on one occasion the front door was struck repeatedly, although no one was there. These phenomena gradually grew in intensity until the evening of August 22nd, when he heard knockings and moaning in the house and finally saw an apparition. He saw it only for a moment. It was walking quickly through the hallway. Dave told me that he had become so frightened by all of this that he ran out of the house! This, apparently, was the last night of the "haunting." Nothing else happened in the house for the next week. Oddly, this last very dramatic night of the "haunting" was the very evening that I had my last dream of returning to the house. So it looks as though somehow, by concentrating on my house, I had actually set up a haunting by long-distance. I don't think that it is coincidence that Dave saw the apparition walking down the hallway, which was the one place in the house I always found myself during my own experiences.

So I guess I succeeded in accomplishing a true psychic *tour de force*. I haunted my own home!

Oh yes. I forgot to mention one other thing. One night, while I was dreaming of being back in the house, I saw Dave's brother sleeping in the spare bedroom. Later I checked and found out that he had indeed spent that night sleeping in the house to keep his brother company . . . and right in that very room.

As I suggested above, these "hauntings-by-the-living" cases strongly imply that all of us have the ability, even while still alive, to set up a haunting. It seems we all possess some sort of psychic force which we can project from our bodies and which can function independently of them. I see no reason why this "force" could not survive our deaths and become permanently latched to our previous homes.

There is even some photographic evidence that these "energy-forms" really do exist. Back in 1907, a French psychic investigator by the name of Hipollyte Baraduc decided to photograph his wife as she lay dying in order to see if he could film the soul leaving her body at death. He photographed her right at the moment of death, and then took several other pictures at regular intervals afterwards. When his photographs were developed, Baraduc was amazed. The photos clearly showed white orbs of light hovering over his wife's body connected by lightening like streaks. These orbs gradually formed into one large white cloud.

Did the French investigator actually photograph the human soul? Or perhaps even a ghost? Later Dr. Baraduc wrote up his bizarre experiment in a curious book entitled, *Mes Morts and leur Manifestations, etc.*

I began this chapter by saying that no one knows for sure what makes a house haunted. The theories I've just discussed are just that . . . unproven ideas. However, it seems that there might well be different types of haunted houses. Some might be caused by the mind of a discarnate entity, as Bozzano believed; while others may be generated by the houses themselves, as Mrs. Sidgwick thought. Yet other hauntings might be produced by even different forces at work. There is probably a little bit of truth in all the theories which have been summarized in this chapter. So we might be making a big mistake by trying to figure out just one theory which can explain what forces are at work in *all* haunted houses. Such an explanation might not even exist.

When I investigate a haunted house, I do so with no bias as to what is causing the disturbances. I merely collect all the facts I can. Then I work out a theory (from among the ones outlined here) which best accounts for the individual case I'm working on, and I apply it to that case and to that case *only*. I don't try to apply what I've learned about the nature of one case automatically to the next haunting I encounter. If anything, a good ghost-hunter must live by one golden rule:

> *Accept* all theories as possible, but *question* each one with skepticism.

8. TIPS FOR FUTURE GHOST-HUNTERS

If you are truly interested in studying haunted houses, the day may come when you will be called upon to investigate one. I can well remember how, when I first became interested in psychical research, the very thought of investigating a haunting or poltergeist thrilled me no end. I could hardly wait for the day when I would be asked to go out, interview witnesses, stay in the haunted house, and perhaps even see a ghost myself. Today, some ten years later, this dream has partially come true. I've investigated dozens of hauntings, both real and fraudulent, and I've even found myself right smack in the middle of a poltergeist attack. I've heard strange noises in at least one haunted house; watched glassware flung about by a poltergeist; and I've spoken with scores of people who have personally witnessed even more amazing things. Although I haven't actually seen a ghost yet, I'm still hoping to see one during some future adventure.

Over the years I've been able to learn a great deal about *how* to investigate a haunted house, too. This is no easy matter, by any means. It's a lot more complicated than just visiting a house, talking with the family members, and drinking a cup of coffee or two while waiting around for some spook to show his face. You really have to be shrewd. You have to know about all the perfectly normal noises a house can produce—such as raps and creaks caused by expanding wood or bad plumbing—which frightened families all too often misinterpret as due to ghostly visitations. You must also be somewhat of a detective. You must look to find if any-one in the house has a motive for pulling a hoax; you must analyze everyone's testimony to make sure all your witnesses agree about what has been going on; and you must know what kinds of experiments to conduct in the house. And, above all else, you have to develop the abili-ty to judge character, since one of your chief duties will be to make some sort of decision as to whether your witnesses are telling you the truth or not. Remember, accept anything as possible, but believe nothing without proof.

Here, then, is a step-by-step guide on how to in-vestigate a haunted house. These few pages are not meant to be an in-depth guide to ghost-hunting, but a set of pointers on how to best handle a haunted house should you ever come across one.

How to Find a Haunted House.

I'm sure that you have all heard that old and very bad joke about the ancient gypsy recipe for chicken soup. First, steal one chicken! The same principle applies to studying haunted houses. Before investigating one, you first have to locate it. But believe it or not, this may not be as difficult as you might think. There are, in fact, many ways to find, or at least to learn about, promising cases.

First of all, check your local papers daily. Reports about ghosts, hauntings, and poltergeists make for good back-page stories. You will be surprised, once you start looking, how many of these strange reports find their way into print. Poltergeist reports seem to be particular-ly newsworthy, and I've come across some of my best cases just by keeping my nose in the morning papers. Also, make sure your friends know of your interest in psychic phenomena. They might come across a likely case now and then in the papers and will no doubt bring it to your attention. I regularly receive "tips" from peo-ple who know of my work and who receive small hometown papers which I would otherwise never see.

If you do come across a good story written up in the press, in all likelihood the address of the house will not be listed. Also, these stories will rarely give very many details about the case. However, the name of the owners of the building or the chief witnesses will usually be printed. So if you wish to pursue the case further, there are two courses of action open to you. First, call the police station located in the district where the case is active. Remember what I said earlier. Families confronted by a haunting or poltergeist generally call in the police first, thinking that perhaps some joker has broken into their houses or that some juvenile delinquent is trying to annoy them. (This is especially true when a family is confronted by a poltergeist outbreak.) Police investigators and officials will usually be very helpful to you, and will often fill you in on unpublished details about the case. If you can convince them that you are not a "nut" and have a scientific interest in the haunting, the police investigators may even put you directly in contact with the distressed family. In some ten years of investigating hauntings, I can only recall one case in which they were less than cooperative.

Your second course of action is to contact the family directly. The best way is by phone or letter. If you have the names of the witnesses but not their addresses, don't worry. Just go down to your city's Hall of Records. There you will find the addresses of anyone who has, or ever had, a telephone with a listed number. Don't forget to make use of the telephone directory as well. Sometimes the simplest method is the best.

Another good way of locating promising cases is to become active in a local psychical research society. Most cities have amateur clubs or groups of this type, and very often their members, or friends of members, will report hauntings to these organizations. When I was Director of Research for the Society for Psychic Research in Los Angeles in 1975, rarely a week went by without somebody calling in to report that his house was haunted. On other occasions, somebody would call in to say that he had a friend stuck with a haunted house. Usually these amateur groups don't have the manpower to go out and investigate all these cases. If you can become active in such a group, and make it well known that you are ready and willing to investigate promising reports, your offer may very well be taken up. In fact, this is one of the ways I first got started myself when I was a teenager.

If you have a college or university in your home town, it might also be a good idea to see if any of the faculty members teaching there are interested in psychical research. (Usually they will be found in the psychology department.) Sometimes people who suddenly find themselves faced with a haunted house will report their problems to a local university in the hope that someone there will be able to help them. (If you recall, when Elke Sommers and Joe Hyams realized their home was haunted they immediately contacted U.C.L.A.) Usually these calls will be turned over to any faculty members available who have shown any interest in the field. However, college teachers are usually very busy people and can't always look into all these reports themselves. So they might just start turning them over to you, if they know of your interest.

Finally, word of mouth is a great way to learn about any likely haunted house in your neighborhood. As your friends, and their friends, learn of your interest in ghost-hunting, you will be surprised how often they will approach you directly. They may tell you of a haunting they know about, or might even ask you to help investigate a case active in their own homes. One investigator at the Psychical Research Foundation (in Durham, North Carolina) even used to contact real estate offices regularly to see if any haunted houses had been recently reported to them. Sure enough, he came across a couple of cases this way.

Of course, you can also do what a friend of mine once did. He went to a few local colleges and put up signs all over the place which read:

WANTED: HAUNTED HOUSES!

He printed his name and phone number underneath. From what I gather, he got all sorts of phone calls in response.

Interviewing Witnesses.

As a ghost-hunter, you have three main responsibilities. First, to learn all you can about the haunting you are investigating. Second, to determine if any normal causes can account for the disturbances reported to you. And third, to decide whether the case is genuine, a misinterpretation of normal occurrences, or a deliberate hoax. Now remember, most of the cases you encounter as a ghost-hunter will probably *not* be genuine. I've found over the years that "strange things" really are going on in about two-thirds of the houses I investigate, but that most of these "phenomena" have quite natural causes and are in no way paranormal. Many other cases I've run into have been out and out frauds.

Now if you want to investigate haunted houses seriously, your best tool-of-the-trade will be your ability to talk and draw information from your witnesses. I rely upon interviewing witnesses more than any other method of investigation. That is; I find it more fruitful to talk with eye-witnesses to a haunting than to merely stay in the house for lengthy periods of time myself (which I have done on occasion), or to bring in psychics, or to conduct complicated experiments. By talking with all the family members in an allegedly haunted house, you can learn just about everything you will need to know about the case in order to help you determine if it is authentic or not. However, interviewing your witnesses is no easy task.

To begin with, there will probably be more than one

or two family members who have witnessed the haunting or poltergeist. You should not interview these people together. Instead, talk to each of them about their experiences in the house privately. In that way, none of the witnesses will be tempted to change his or her story to make it fit in or better correspond with the stories the others are reporting. They will be forced to rely solely upon their own memories. Then you can go back and compare the various accounts you have received, and see whether or not they match up. As you interview your informants, it is best to have each family member relate to you the *first* odd phenomenon he or she ever encountered in the house. Then go on to the second incident, and so forth. This will give you a good history of the haunting, and not just a jumbled-up series of ghost stories. As I said, repeat this procedure with each of the family members. After you have collected all the testimony, you can then start analyzing your case by asking yourself a series of questions:

First, does all the testimony add up? It is important for you to make sure that all your witnesses are telling you similar stories. If one witness claims that mysterious footsteps have been heard walking about the house nightly, other family members should be complaining about similar manifestations. If the family members come up with *different* stories about what is going on in their home, this should alert you to the possibility that they are either making up tales or only imagining that the house in haunted. Secondly, you should ask yourself, have any of the haunting phenomena been witnessed by more than one person at the same time? If a case is genuine, usually some of the manifestations will have been collectively seen or heard. For instance, maybe three people will have heard mysterious footsteps in the house at the same time. It is always best to have as many independent accounts of the *same* incident as possible. Check out these incidents carefully. If two people claim that on one occasion a fish bowl came sailing through the air, make sure both of them have described the event to you in the same way. For instance, both witnesses should agree as to where the bowl was originally positioned in the house and about the direction and speed at which it moved. If both your informants agree on these points, then you can be sure the incident actually occurred in just the way they reported it. But if they disagree then you cannot accept the incident as evidence of anything. You must conclude that the incident was very poorly observed. For instance, if only one of your witnesses claims that the bowl came flying out of an empty room, you cannot accept his word for it. If, however, *both* witnesses agree that it flew from an unoccupied room, this indicates that you may be up against a genuine case.

I do not mean to say, though, that everyone's testimony should be 100% consistent with everyone else's. After all, some people have better memories and powers of observation than others. You should expect a small number of inconsistencies within your reports, but not obvious or glaring ones. That is why it is absolutely necessary for you to interview your witnesses independently.

Taking down all this testimony, by the way, presents certain problems in itself. Generally, there are three ways you can record your interviews. You can make notes while talking with the family members; or have them write out detailed descriptions of their experiences; or tape record their testimony. You will probably find that taping will be the easiest and most efficient method for note-taking. And little casette recorders aren't very expensive. On the other hand, writing out your notes from dictation is difficult and time-consuming. You might find yourself paying more attention to your writing than to your informants. It is, of course, nice to have neatly typed or written statements from your witnesses about their experiences. However, people will usually give you much more detailed accounts if they can recount them verbally into a tape machine. Simply speaking, it is easier to describe an experience verbally than to sit down and laboriously write it all out. Also, as your witness describes his experiences you can stop him at any point and ask for either more information or ask him to clarify some remark he has made.

Now that you have all the testimony recorded, your work really begins!

First, map out the history of the case event by event. Make sure you know the date of each incident and which family members witnessed it. You can do this by taking a sheet of paper and dividing it into three columns. In the first, give a date. In the next, describe the incident. And in the third, record who was at home at the time and experienced the phenomenon, and where he was located in the house. You might have a list of twenty incidents or so.

Second, you should draw up a floorplan of the house and mark off where every member of the household was standing or sitting at the time of each incident. Do this for each and every occurrence. As you go through this procedure, it may become obvious to you whether the case is genuine or not. If, for instance, a family member reported that on one occasion a bottle came flying down the hallway stairs, check to see where everyone in the house was positioned at the critical moment. If everyone was sitting together in the living room when the incident occurred, it was probably a genuine psychic happening. But if everyone was in the living room except a young child—who just happened to be upstairs at the time—it is possible that this family member threw the object himself.

Third, now check over all your maps. Check to see if one person always seemed to be unaccounted for, or was by himself and unwatched, whenever the haunting supposedly acted up. This would indicate a hoax.

If you do suspect a hoax, you can sometimes prove it to yourself just by interviewing your witnesses a little more thoroughly. See if they change their stories around. I have learned over the years that people who have experienced genuine psychic phenomena in their homes will stick to their stories no matter how hard you try to shake them. However, people who are faking, or just making up tall stories, will usually try to tell you thing they *think* you want to hear. So if I suspect a fraud, I will deliberately "bait" my witnesses and get them to admit to all sorts of ridiculous things. For instance, ghosts seen in conventional haunted houses rarely walk about shrieking. Likewise, while many people trapped in haunted houses will complain that certain areas of the house seem unusually cold to them, I know of no cases on record where witnesses have felt hot spots in these buildings. So if I think a case I'm investigating is a hoax, I will deliberately tell the family member that ghosts often shriek and that hot spots are commonly found in haunted places. Often the hoaxers will grab the bait and will start telling me that they have indeed encountered shrieking ghosts and hot spots, or will complain of these very manifestations during the following weeks!

I have also used this trick on people who, to my knowledge, have witnessed genuine haunting phenomena. They have never picked up these suggestions and reported them back to me.

There are other ways you can trick a hoaxer into exposing himself. For instance, you can get all the family members to engage in a "rap" session about what they have witnessed in the house. If your informants have not been telling you the truth, they will probably start trying to outdo each other with the best "ghost stories" that they can think up. And these stories can be pretty wild. I once investigated a case in which the entire family originally claimed only that a ghost walked about their house almost every night. It was clear from talking to them, though, that they were just out for publicity. So I got them into a talk session. By the end of the afternoon, the family members were claiming that fires were being set in the house, that furniture often flew about, and that mysterious bell-like chimes and clangings were being heard all night! As the family members tried to impress me and each other with these dumb stories, one of them even claimed that some psychic force had lifted him into the air!

Examining the House.

Many people who think their homes are haunted are often only misinterpreting perfectly normal sounds and phenomena. One of your jobs as you check out a supposedly haunted house is to see whether there are any leaky or rattling pipes which may be causing these odd noises. Electrical malfunctions, plumbing, the effects of the rain and wind, and all sorts of other natural problems can also convince a family that they are being haunted. However, many of these cases are dead giveaways.

For example, if the "ghostly noises" reported to you by a family always break out at the same time and in the same part of the house, this usually indicates that they have a normal physical cause. A long time ago I investigated a house in which strange soft "tapping sounds" were heard nightly. They always broke out in one bedroom of the old house, and the owners were sure a ghost was loose. They called a friend of mine to look into the matter and I went along. It took me about five minutes or so to figure out what was making the noise. After listening to the family's spine-chilling accounts of the ghostly knockings, I crawled under the house and located a water pipe, which was of course connected to a water heater, running under the bedroom and along the same spot where the noises were heard. This could hardly be a coincidence, I thought. So I asked the family members to stay in the "haunted room"and call out when they heard the tappings. In the meantime, I went into the kitchen and started tapping on the water heater.

At that same time, the family called out that the rappings were starting up. Obviously, the heater was dripping water inside the tank and the sound of the "plop-plop-plop" was echoing through the pipe and could therefore be heard in the bedroom. Case solved!

As I just indicated, gas heaters and faulty electrical work can cause all sorts of odd manifestations, from creating fierce pounding sounds to making lights switch on and off. Even the water pressure in a kitchen faucet can pull some mighty nifty tricks. Pressure can build up so much that the faucet will begin to leak, as though it actually turned on by itself.

If you should come across a case in which electrical disturbances are the *only* phenomena reported by the witnesses, more often than not you will be able to find a normal explanation for the "haunting." Just recommend that the family call in a good electrician or plumber. However, be alert. Sometimes electrical and other seemingly normal malfunctions can actually be the first signs that a poltergeist is about to break. (For a good example of this type of case, check back to the Rosenheim case which was summarized in Chapter 5.)

There are also other features of a house you should always check out. What kind of soil is it built on? Are there any underground rivers or bodies of water nearby? Or any old mine shafts which have been sealed off? All of these geological factors can make a house shift slightly on its foundation, thus causing noises to occur inside or even cause furniture to move about. If, for instance, your witnesses tell you that their haunting is most active after rain storms, check to see if the house is built on ground containing a lot of clay or chalk. As this type of soil resettles after a storm, it can put stress on a house which may then begin producing all sorts of grunts, groans, creaks, and moans. You should also check the area around the house. You will be surprised what you will sometimes discover.

For example, Andrew Green, a well-known British investigator, tells the following story in his book *Ghost Hunting:*

> Several campers in a small clearing in a wood had frequently and regularly heard what they described as "a sort of whistling moan", which they attributed to "a ghost". It was found that some yards away a small dip in the ground was partially filled with household and some industrial rubbish. A few feet further on the ground fell away to a treeless valley. Although a few of the braver ones had carried out a rough search for the phantom, they had been unsuccessful, though they had learnt of some weird stories from local residents.

Green goes on to say that shortly afterwards a ghost-hunter arrived on the scene. He discovered that the weird noises were only heard when the wind was blowing from a certain direction. He then checked out the junk pile and found an old pair of metal cylinders lying on the ground. These had acted like crude pipe-organs. When the wind blew through them, they produced a curious whining sound.

Actually, if ghostly disturbances are only observed by a family after or during storms, these phenomena will usually be of a normal nature.

Andrew Green also cites one possible normal explanation for those strange footsteps so often heard in haunted houses. While his explanation cannot account for all of these curious cases, no doubt some "phantom footstep" mysteries have perfectly natural solutions. As Green explains:

> One of the causes of "phantom footsteps", I believe, is the regular contraction of floorboards, starting from the wall nearest the heat from a fireplace, a night storage unit, or a radiator. Once one board con-

tracts and creaks, it releases the pressure on the adjoining board which then also contracts and creaks. The process and sound travels across the floor at such regular intervals that "footsteps" are very often thought to have been heard.

Checking Out the History of a House.

If you do come across what you consider to be a genuine haunted house, you may want to learn about its past history. One way to do this is by checking with previous tenants and owners. You can locate their names in public files. Every owner of a house will at least know the name of the previous residents, and he may be willing to turn this information over to you. You might then want to write to these people and see if they are willing to discuss the house with you. And you may find out that they also witnessed strange goings-on in the house.

I should warn you, though, that sometimes the people you contact will be very uncooperative. Always remember that most of them will be terrified by the thought of ridicule or bad publicity. This is especially true of the families actually confronting the haunting. It is your responsibility as a ghost-hunter to assure them that their testimony and the information they give you will be kept confidential. Your pledge of secrecy will often assure them of your good faith, and they will be more cooperative because of it.

If a house has had a long history of haunting phenomena associated with it, it is a good indication that the house is genuinely haunted. On the other hand, check to see if any alterations (such as remodeling or additions) were done on the house and seem related to the time the haunting first broke out. If so, this could be indicating that the structural supports of the house were weakened at that time, and might be causing the house itself to produce odd noises which were never noticed before.

Of course, you should also try to learn if any tragic

events ever took place in the house. If there are any elderly people who have lived in the neighborhood for many years, they may know something about the house's history. However, your main job is to determine whether or not a haunting is genuine. So don't be too discouraged if you cannot discover the *cause* of the hauntings you come across in the course of your investigations.

Experiments to Conduct in a Haunted House and Methods of Observation.

An ideal ghost-hunter should be equipped with all sorts of fancy gadgets as he makes his investigation. If you happen to be rich, that's no problem. You could bring in cameras to continually film the house in hopes of photographing either the ghost or perhaps some object floating about. You could even set up T.V. monitors all through the building. Then you could sit in one room, and still watch what is going on every place else. You could also bring in delicate thermometers to check if any odd temperature changes are taking place. Unfortunately, few ghost-hunters are so nicely equipped. However, even an amateur can conduct a few simple experiments in a haunted house or at least carry out a thorough investigation.

The simplest method of actively investigating a haunted house is to just sit and wait there until something happens! If phenomena seem to be breaking out daily, you should plan on spending some time just visiting the home. If the haunting or poltergeist is genuine, you will usually find your host willing to have you there. Once I stayed at a haunted house for three days straight. (I learned a valuable lesson from this case—always carry a sleeping bag in the trunk of your car!) While visiting a haunted house, though, you must do more than just sit around like a dead log. You must be alert at all times. Also, you must keep track of everyone in the house. If somebody leaves the building or walks from one room to another, you must make a written or tape-recorded note to that effect. This way, you will be in a position to know the exact whereabouts of everyone should anything happen during your stay.

Another important rule of ghost-hunting, especially during poltergeist attacks, is to keep the family members under constant observation while you are staying at the house. Let's say, for instance, that an ashtray flies out of the kitchen while you are investigating a case. If everyone in the house is sitting with you in the living room, then you know that no living hand could have thrown it. But if the family members are all in different rooms— and you haven't kept track of their whereabouts—there is simply no way you can authenticate the incident.

Keeping the family under constant guard does pose certain difficulties, though. After all, you don't want to act like a kidnapper keeping check on a group of hostages. You have to be subtle. If the family feels that you distrust them or expect fraud, they may easily become offended and ask you to leave. And you can hardly blame them. Instead, you must constantly engage the family members in conversation, or suggest politely that they not move around too much. People won't move about unnecessarily when you are talking with them, so I often keep up a constant chatter while visiting a haunted house or encourage my witnesses to tell me all about themselves. You might also remind the families that you are there to investigate their problem and need their full cooperation. It also helps if you happen to have a friend who is also well-versed in ghost-hunting. It is very difficult for just one person to control and observe a family of five people. Two investigators can do the job more efficiently. Over the last several years, I have always asked Raymond Bayless to accompany me on my adventures and Raymond also requests me to help out on his cases. By stationing ourselves in different rooms of an allegedly haunted house, we have often found ourselves in a better position to determine if a case is genuine or not. During one poltergeist case we investigated a few years ago, Raymond was sitting in the kitchen one morning with two of the household members. At the same time I was in the living room with another member of the family, a young girl around whom the poltergeist was centering. Suddenly a spoon came flying out of the hallway and landed in the living room. Had Raymond not been with the other two members of the family at that moment, I would never have been able to authenticate this particular incident as a genuine PK occurrence.

Another method of testing out a haunted house is to bring some animals along with you. Sometimes animals will act strangely in haunted places. If you recall, Rose Despard's little dog often acted very frightened when the Cheltenham ghost was on the prowl. Likewise, our dog Duchess seemed to be a pretty good "ghost detector" herself. I could quote many other similar cases as well. You can also check out *particular parts* of a house to see if they are haunted by using animal detectors. If a certain room in a haunted house seems to be the seat of the haunting, you might wish to see if your pets will act strangely in that room. One parapsychologist I know, Mr. Graham Watkins of Durham, North Carolina, regularly uses animals in just this way during his investigations.

Graham once told me about a haunted house in Kentucky which he checked out a few years ago. A suicide had once been committed in one of the bedrooms. Since Graham is an expert on animal behavior, he decided when he first visited the house to take along a dog, a cat, a rat, and a rattlesnake! He let the animals into the haunted room one by one. The dog was the first to enter. It immediately snarled, turned around and tried to escape from the room. Once out in the hallway, it refused to reenter the room no matter how hard the experimenters coaxed him. The cat acted just as frightened when it was carried into the room by its owner. It leaped to the

floor, turned towards a chair situated in a corner of the
room and hissed at it continually for several minutes.
Although the rat did not act at all oddly in the room,
Graham told me, his rattlesnake sure did. As soon as it
was placed in the center of the room, housed inside a
small glass case, it acted extremely alarmed. It, too,
looked immediately toward the chair at which the cat
had hissed and assumed an "attack" position as though
ready to strike at it. None of the four animals, Graham
added when he told me about the investigation, acted
strangely anywhere else in the house.

As I indicated before, I don't recommend bringing
psychics into an allegedly haunted house. However if
you already know a good deal about the background of
a house, you may want to see if a psychic will come up
with similar information. Of course, while a good way to
discover if your psychic has genuine ESP ability, this
course of action may not actually tell you very much
about the haunting. Some years ago, you see, a British
parapsychologist whom I know very well investigated a
poltergeist which was rampaging in a small English
town. He brought in a well-known psychic to help him
get to the cause of the haunting. Indeed, the psychic was
able to psychically and correctly trace some of the
house's former history, and even came up with the exact
name of a former resident. Later, though, the parapsychologist discovered that the poltergeist was being
caused by the young son of the tenants, who was unin-
tentionally using his PK powers to produce the disturbances. So while the psychic's impressions about the
house were correct, they had absolutely nothing to do
with the haunting!

Nonetheless, you may want to carry out a little experiment similar to the one Dr. Moss conducted while she
was investigating the Elke Sommers house, as recounted
in Chapter 2. If you have some friends who are psychic,
or who think they are, you might have them visit the
house one by one. Give each of them a list of words

which could possibly describe the ghost or haunting.
Have them simply check off those words which they feel
apply to the ghost. You might also have all the family
members carry out the same procedure. Then you can
check to see if your friends generally agree with the family, or among themselves, about the nature of the ghost.
This group of words is called an "adjective checklist,"
and the following words should be placed on your list:

active	dignified	mature
affectionate	distrustful	meek
aggressive	emotional	mischievous
alert	enterprising	noisy
aloof	fearful	obliging
anxious	forgiving	patient
apathetic	friendly	peaceable
arrogant	gentle	quiet
bitter	greedy	rigid
calm	headstrong	shy
changeable	helpful	stern
cold	humorous	strong
complaining	immature	submissive
confused	impatient	tolerant
contented	impulsive	trusting
cruel	independent	vindictive
demanding	irritable	warm
despondent	jolly	weak
determined	leisurely	

You can also use psychics to ascertain if any area of
a house is particularly haunted. Just carry out a little
experiment such as the one Dr. Gertrude Schmeidler
conducted when she investigated her friend's New York
house and which was discussed in the previous chapter.
Draw up a floorplan of the house and ask your psychic
friends to visit there and mark off any areas where they
can feel the ghost's presence particularly strongly. Have
the family members do the same thing. If you find your

witnesses and psychics agreeing that certain rooms are the most active centers of the haunting, this information will be of some use to you. For one thing, it will indicate where you should concentrate your attention while staying in the house yourself.

If, however, you are more gadget-minded, you might like to try some more sophisticated types of experiments. You might take along thermometers and place them throughout the house to see if they will mysteriously change temperature readings. You might also seal off all air vents, windows, and doors to any room which has been the scene of active disturbances, and then hang mobiles from the ceiling. If any type of "psychic energy" becomes active in the room, these paper hangings may start to swing. But be very sure that no air drafts are getting into the room.

Many other suggestions for the "instrumental" study of haunted houses can be found in an article by Dr. Charles Tart, a psychologist at the University of California at Davis, entitled "Application of Instrumentation in the Investigation of Haunting and Poltergeist Cases." This interesting paper was published in the July, 1965 issue of the *Journal* of the American Society for Psychical Research. Dr. Tart suggests how to use photocells, thermisters, tape recorders, strain gauges, and other devices in the study of haunted houses. However, these procedures are too complicated to go into here.

Conclusion

A ghost-hunter certainly has to be armed with many tools and tricks of the trade. He must know what he is looking for, what types of phenomena he should and should not expect to be reported to him; he should be able to conduct proper interviews, and he should know how to conduct simple experiments right on the spot. However, your most important tool will be *you yourself*. You must use *your* mind and judgment, *your* cunning, and *your* powers of observation as you look into a case.

No gadgets or raw knowledge will help you to carry out an investigation successfully if you are lacking in any of these abilities or personal qualities.

Remember, too, that a psychic investigator is very much like a doctor or a minister. While investigating a haunting or poltergeist, always remember that you have been called in by a distressed family because they need your help, more than for any other reason. You will no doubt be confronted by a lot of very frightened people as you carry out your work. So one of your chief responsibilities will be to assure your witnesses that they have nothing to fear, that many families have found themselves in similar circumstances, and that modern science and parapsychology are now beginning to understand these strange phenomena. Remind them, too, that these phenomena are only frightening because they seem so strange; not because they are in any way evil or harmful. It is my own feeling that a ghost-hunter's first and foremost obligation is to help the families with whom he comes into contact to deal mentally with what they are experiencing. So you must talk with your witnesses as one friend to another, and help them to understand a bit about psychic phenomena. Try to make them understand what they are confronting, just as you yourself understand a little about the nature of these phenomena. We usually do not fear that which we understand.

In closing, then, let me say that it took me several years of ghost-hunting before I finally stumbled onto a genuine case. So try not to be discouraged if your first investigations don't turn up very much. I am sure that you will encounter many hoaxes. You will also no doubt meet a lot of very strange or scared people who—for all sorts of reasons—have erroneously come to believe that their homes are haunted. It is easy to become downhearted. But if you keep on investigating every case you hear about, follow up every tip you find in the newspapers, and keep actively looking for good cases, I am sure that you will eventually find yourself right smack in the middle of a genuine case. There were times when I thought that day would never come, but I was wrong. So never give up your quest. You won't be sorry.

Good h(a)unting!

GLOSSARY

Agent. A person who "sends" during an ESP test, or who produces psychic phenomena.

Apparition. A non-physical or only partially material form which resembles a human being or animal.

Clairvoyance. The extrasensory awareness of a physical object or event; such as "seeing" into a closed box or "knowing" what is happening miles away.

Dematerialize. To vanish into thin air.

Discarnate entity. The surviving spirit of a once living person.

Extrasensory perception. A process during which information comes into the mind and body but is not channeled through or received by sight, hearing, taste, touch, or smell. Also a general term for telepathy, clairvoyance, and seeing into the future. Usually abreviated as *ESP*.

Ghost. An apparition seen over and over, usually in the same place.

Haunted house. A house in which psychic phenomena occur over and over again, over many years.

Haunting. Any place, including a house, where psychic phenomena occur over and over again, and over a long period of time.

Levitate. To lift something into the air by psychic means. The phenomenon is called *levitation*.

Materialization. The formation of matter out of thin air; or the sudden appearance of a physical object out of the air.

Parapsychology. That branch of science which studies

psychic phenomena, such as ESP and psycho-kinesis.

Parapsychologist. A scientist or person specially trained to study psychic phenomena.

Phantom. See *apparition.*

PK. See *psychokinesis.*

Poltergeist. A type of haunting, usually focusing on a person rather than a place, which causes recurrent PK phenomena.

Poltergeist agent. A person who can produce a poltergeist, or around whom the poltergeist centers.

Precognition. ESP of the future or of a future event.

Psi. Any type of psychic occurrence. (In other words, *psi phenomena*).

Psychic. A person with ESP and/or PK abilities; or descriptive of such a person or event (such as a *psychic* person or a *psychic* phenomenon).

Psychic investigator. A person who investigates psychic phenomena. *Also,* psychical investigator.

Psychic phenomena. A general term for any or all psychic occurences (such as ESP, PK, hauntings, poltergeists, etc.).

Psychical research. An older term for parapsychology.

Psychokinesis. The direct influence of the mind or will on a physical object. *Also,* PK or mind-over-matter.

Psychometry. The practice of gaining ESP impression from touching physical objects.

Subject. A person being tested for psychic abilities.

Telekinesis. Another term for psychokinesis.

Telepathy. Perceiving or responding to the thoughts of others, as in mind-reading.

Teleportation. The passage of a physical object *through* another physical object.

SUGGESTED READING*

Bardens, Dennis. *Ghosts and Hauntings. New York: Taplinger, 1965 (2).

Bayless, Raymond. Animal Ghosts. New Hyde Park: University Books, 1970 (2).

Bayless, Raymond. *The Enigma of the Poltergeist. West Nyack: Parker, 1967 (2).

Ebon, Martin, ed. *True Experiences with Ghosts. New York: New American Library, 1968 (1).

Haining, Peter. Ghosts: The Illustrated History. New York: Macmillan, 1975 (2).

Knight, David. *Poltergeists: Hauntings and the Haunted. Philadelphia: J.B. Lippincott, 1972 (1).

MacKenzie, Andrew. *Apparitions and Ghosts. London: Barker, 1971 (2).

MacKenzie, Andrew. A Gallery of Ghosts. New York: Taplinger, 1972 (2).

Owen, A.R.G. Can We Explain the Poltergeist? New York: Garrett, 1964 (3).

Owen, A.R.G. and Sims, Victor. Science and the Spook. New York: Garrett, 1971, (2).

Rogo, D. Scott. *An Experience of Phantoms. New York: Taplinger, 1974 (2).

Rogo, D. Scott. *The Poltergeist Experience. New York: Penguin, 1978 (2).

---

*These books are labeled according to reading level: (1) Easy or non-technical. (2) Medium difficulty. (3) Recommended for more advanced reading. Books marked with an asterisk (*) are available in paperback.

Roll, W.G. *The Poltergeist*. New York: New American Library, 1973 (3).

Smith, Susy. *Ghosts Around the House*. New York: World, 1970 (2).

Smith, Susy. *Haunted Houses for the Millions*. Los Angeles: Scherborne Press, (1).

Smyth, Frank. *Ghosts and Poltergeists*. Garden City: Doubleday, 1976 (1).

REFERENCES

Chapter 1

CASE	DATE	SOURCE
Christ Episcopal Church	1968	Rauscher, William. *The Spiritual Frontier.* Garden City: Doubleday, 1975.
Queen's Head Inn	1953	MacKenzie, Andrew. *Apparitions and Ghosts.* London: Arthur Barker, 1971.
Grandpa Bull	1932	MacKenzie, Andrew. *A Gallery of Ghosts.* New York: Taplinger, 1972.
Villa of Comeada, Portugal	1919	Flammarion, Camille. *Haunted Houses.* New York: Appleton, 1924.
Eagle Rock House	1944	Bayless, Raymond. *The Enigma of the Poltergeist.* West Nyack: Parker, 1967.
S.S. Watertown	1924	Rogo, D. Scott. *An Experience of Phantoms.* New York: Taplinger, 1974.
Raynham Hall	1835; 1936	Stevens, William O. *Unbidden Guests.* New York: Dodd & Mead, 1946.

Chapter 2

CASE	DATE	SOURCE
The Cheltenham Haunting	1882-89	Collins, B. Abdy: *The Cheltenham Ghost.* London: Psychic Press, 1948.
Borley Rectory	?-1939	Price, Harry. *The Most Haunted House in England.* London: Harrap, 1940 Price, Harry, *The End of Borley Rectory.* London: Harrap, 1946

CASE	DATE	SOURCE
The Philadel-phia Duplex	1972	Pierce, Henry. "RSPK Phenomena Observed Independently by Two Families." *Journal:* Amer. Soc. for Psych. Res. 67 (1973): 86-101.
Elke Sommers's House	1965	Ebon, Martin. *True Experiences with Ghosts.* New York, New American Library, 1968.
		Moss, Thelma and Schmeidler, Gertrude. "Quantitative Investigation of a 'Haunted House' with Sensitives and a Control Group," *Journal:* Amer. Soc. for Psych. Res. 62 (1968): 399-410.
The Norfolk Apartment Complex	1967	Joines, W.T. "Investigations in Norfolk and Long Island," *Theta,* Winter (1968): 3-4
New Jersey House	1972	Rosenberg, Robert. "A Haunting in New Jersey," *Theta,* Winter-Spring (1974): 17-18.
Maryland Haunting	1973	Eisler, William. "A Haunting in Maryland," *Theta,* Fall (1974): 1-3.

Note: Summaries of other cases investigated by the Psychical Research Foundation may be found in a previous book of mine, *An Experience of Phantoms* (New York: Taplinger, 1974).

Chapter 3

Further details may be found in two previous books of mine, *An Experience of Phantoms* (New York: Taplinger, 1974) and *In Search of the Unknown* (New York: Taplinger, 1976).

Chapter 4

CASE	DATE	SOURCE
The *Ivan Vassilli*	1903	Gaddis, Vincent. *Invisible Horizons.* Radnor: Penn. Chilton, 1965

The Le Leau Haunting	1930	Le Leau, Esther. "An Unusual and Recurrent Experience," *Journal:* Amer. Soc. for Psych. Res. 45: (1951) 158-65.
The Machías Ghost	1966	Smith, Susy. *Ghosts Around the House.* Cleveland: World, 1966.
The Witherspoon Haunting	1967	Smith, Susy. *Ghosts Around the House.* Cleveland: World, 1966.
The Brooklyn House	1894-98	Wood, Elizabeth G. "Experiences in a House," *Proceedings:* Amer. Soc. for Psych. Res. 14 (1920): 360-418

Chapter 5

CASE	DATE	SOURCE
The Thornton Heath Poltergeist	1939	Fodor, Nandor. *On the Trail of the Poltergeist.* New York: Citadel, 1958.
The Rosenheim Case	1967-68	Bender, Hans. "Modern Poltergeist Research." In Beloff, John, ed., *New Directions in Parapsychology.* London: Elek, 1974.
The Seaford Case	1958	Roll, W.G. *The Poltergeist.* New York: New American Library, 1973

Chapter 6

CASE	DATE	SOURCE
The Baylesses' experiences	1972, 1975, 1976	These reports are based on material given me by the Baylesses in 1977.
Mr. Landau's experience	1955	MacKenzie, Andrew. *The Unexplained.* New York: Abelard-Schuman, 1970.
The phantom Great Dane	1926	Daniels, Helen and Pierson, Jocelyn. "Case of an Animal Apparition,"

Journal: American Soc. for Psych. Res.
35 (1941): 92-97.

| The return of "Butch" | 1950 | Reported in the *Journal:* Amer. Soc. for Psych. Res. 46: (1952) 154-57. |

Chapter 7

CASE	DATE	SOURCE
Dr. Schmeidler's friend	1965	Schmeidler, Gertrude. "Quantitative Investigation of a Haunted House," *Journal:* Am. Soc. for Psych. Resch. 60 (1966): 193-49.
The ghost by the window	——	Green, Celia/McCreery, Charles. *Apparitions.* London: Hamish Hamilton, 1975.
The house of Dr. E.	1886	——*Proceedings:* Amer. Soc. for Psych. Resch 10 (1894): 358 et. seq.

Chapter 8

For further information on how to investigate hauntings, the following publications are recommended:

The Society for Psychical Research (1 Adam and Eve Mews, London W8, England) publishes a booklet on the subject, "Notes for Investigators of Spontaneous Cases" and is available through them. Some guidelines for investigating ghosts and poltergeists, including a set of interview questions, may be found in an appendix to W.G. Roll's *The Poltergeist* (New York: New American Library, 1973). Another handy book is Andrew Green's *Ghost Hunting: A Practical Guide* (London: Garnstone Press, 1973).

D. SCOTT ROGO is an ideal person to write a book on haunted houses. An active ghost-hunter himself, he read his first book on haunted houses when he was twelve, investigated his first one when he was seventeen, and moved into a haunted house himself when he was twenty-one.

As well as being a writer, Mr. Rogo has held several positions with leading parapsychology institutions throughout the country. He has been a visiting research consultant for the Psychical Research Foundation in Durham, North Carolina; a visiting researcher at the Brooklyn-based Maimonides Medical Center's division of parapsychology and psychophysics; and director of research for the Southern California Society for Psychical Research.

In addition to *The Haunted House Handbook,* he is author of some dozen books of parapsychology, including two previous works on hauntings: *An Experience of Phantoms* and *The Poltergeist Experience.*

He is a lifelong resident of Los Angeles, where his current residence is—unfortunately—not haunted.